Voyage of the Capek

George T. Hahn

For more on the epic science fiction series, go to the official website,

www.tauceti2.com

Contents

1.	Leaving Trist	1
2.	Moving In	6
3.	Vacation's Over	9
4.	Down on the Farm	13
5.	Conversations	17
6.	Party Plans	20
7.	A Run Through the Grass	24
8.	A Quick Stop	28
9.	All Quiet	32
10.	Madelaine vs. Karel	36
11.	When in Doubt	40
12.	Chance of Success	44
13.	Friendly Conversation?	48
14.	Ron's Speech	52
15.	Maneuvering	56
16.	Karel Acts	59
17.	Karel Miscalculates	63
18.	Growing Conflict	67
19.	Accident on Deck Ten	71
20.	An Arrival at Sirius	75
21.	Suspicions	77

22. Miranda's Request   80

23. Desperate Times   84

24. Desperate Measures   88

25. Leaving Sirius   92

26. Awakening   94

27. A New Home   98

28. A Light in the Sky   101

A Final Word   105

Excerpt from "The Methuselah Conspirators"   106

Excerpt from "The Ambassador: The Lost Colony"   115

Leaving Trist

R ON RIGNEY STARED AT the Astrarium, shoulders hunched and hands clenched behind him, feeling every one of his eighty-nine years. His wife, Tiffany, leaned against him, gripping his arm. Karel, the main computer for the library ship Capek, used the huge Astrarium screen to show the crippled Benjamin Sepulveda, motionless in space a mile away. The shuttle it had carried to Trist drifted away with its dead crew, the broken cooling fin from the Benjamin Sepulveda still protruding from its hull.

Ron looked at his wife and sighed. She had wanted to leave Trist so badly, but what was she thinking now? They hadn't meant to hurt anyone. Karel had used the gravity tractor missile to delay the shuttle, not cause it to lose control and collide with the *Benjamin Sepulveda*. "Change the view to show Trist, Karel," Ron said.

"Yes, Administrator." The computer immediately changed the view to show the greenish sphere that had been their home. Unlike Earth, the green tint extended over the entire globe, not just land areas, because the color came from the atmosphere and its chlorine. The tunnels of the colony were somewhere under that poisonous atmosphere, still populated by all the friends and family they were leaving behind.

"*Benjamin Sepulveda* First Officer Madelaine Chandler has left her room and is moving toward the bridge," Karel reported.

"Why don't you go back to our quarters and rest," Ron told Tiffany.

Tiffany nodded, gave him a tentative smile, and left the bridge. Madelaine Chandler arrived seconds later. He watched her advance between the rows of equipment that filled the bridge, striding forward with all the confidence of someone used to command. Madelaine was an attractive woman in her mid-forties, the ranking officer among the *Benjamin Sepulveda* crew since Captain McCabe had opted to take one of the Capek shuttles down to Trist.

"We have a few things to discuss," Madelaine said as she reached Ron's chair.

Ron sat before one of the many instrument stations on the bridge, there more for monitoring than control since the entire ship was automated. He motioned to the chair at the station next to his. "We do. Have a seat."

The woman appeared calm but solemn, and Ron hoped that meant she wasn't there to protest again about being on *Capek*. They would have to work together for a long time, the rest of their lives, and Madelaine's attitude seemed to show that she knew that.

"First, now that we're about to be under way, perhaps you could tell me what you hope to gain by taking this ship to Tau Ceti."

Ron grimaced. "I wouldn't gain anything. Earth would just come to get us. We're not going to Tau Ceti."

Madelaine jolted back in the chair, and Ron knew it hadn't occurred to the officer that they might go elsewhere. "Where?" Madelaine asked after a pause.

"The star is called 82 G. Eridani. A planet slightly smaller than Trist was discovered within the water zone back in 2067. The planet has a breathable atmosphere, according to spectrographic studies."

"That must mean a longer trip. How long?"

"It will take us about six years to get there."

Madelaine shook her head. "Only six years? Even Tau Ceti isn't that close."

Ron smiled. "Karel's robots have been busy. Using data from the latest Earth technology updates, Karel started improving its drives about six months ago. Its cruising speed is now nine-tenths light speed instead of six-tenths. Thirteen years will go by, but time dilation will make that about six for us."

"And you hope to hide there?"

Ron tried to keep his voice level. "We hope to make it our new home. Something more hospitable than Trist."

The image on the Astrarium screen wavered and went black. A fraction of a second later, a field of stars appeared with one star circled. "I have engaged Stenhouse Drive," Karel said. "Since I can't display actual images while the drive is on, I have displayed a stored image of the constellation Eridanus and marked our destination."

"Thank you, Karel," Ron said.

"And what is our part in this mad scheme?" Madelaine asked.

"We hope you will join our community, of course. I don't see where you have any other option. I'm sorry about that, but I assume you would agree that is better than dying on the *Benjamin Sepulveda*."

Madelaine frowned. "A choice we wouldn't have had to make if you hadn't attacked my ship."

"Karel fired the missile in self-defense. I didn't give the order. However, I think I can confidently assure you that the intent was to delay boarding by the shuttle you were carrying. There was no desire to damage the shuttle or your ship."

Madelaine shook her head. "I don't understand. Why didn't you just ask for a transfer back to Earth or to Pitcairn? Why steal this ship and abandon your people?"

Madelaine's question startled Ron. Why hadn't they asked to be transferred? He never even considered it, and no one else had suggested it either. He thought back. Karel originally voiced the possibility of moving *Capek* to Pitcairn, the colonized planet at Tau Ceti. Did other options not occur to the computer, or did the computer have its own reasons for wanting to relocate?

Ron had visited Pitcairn, and knew of the Pitcairners' struggles against Terran dominance. He had traveled with Patrick Malley, his counterpart on Pitcairn, to the Colonial Reorganization Conference where the Western Alliance made plain their desire to control Pitcairn. He had been there when the Pitcairners discovered that the Western Alliance's real goal was to control *Asimov*, the library ship orbiting Pitcairn, and its conscious computer, all in pursuing the Methuselah Project.

When Pitcairn defeated the Western Alliance by maneuvering the Western Alliance into granting it independence, attention turned to Trist and Karel Capek, the *Capek* computer who had also become conscious. The investigations proposed by the Methuselah Project would have been dangerous to Karel, so the computer certainly had reasons for leaving Trist and the reach of the Western Alliance.

Ron's experiences made him cynical about Earth's intentions, and perhaps that was why he had so easily fixated on Karel's plan, ignoring possible simpler alternatives. His desperation about Tiffany's depression may have also clouded his thoughts.

"You don't seem to have an answer to my question," Madelaine said. "It's not too late to turn around."

"That would not be advisable," Karel said. Its voice was not quite monotone, but easily recognized as that of a computer. It was, of course, listening to the conversation. It heard them almost anywhere on the ship, although its ability to speak was limited to the bridge and to computer terminals in other areas of the massive starship. "The Western Alliance will certainly want to punish you for what happened to Benjamin Sepulveda."

Madelaine gave Ron a suspicious glare. "You said that the computer attacked *Benjamin Sepulveda*."

It took an effort for Ron to summon the energy to answer Madelaine. "You know that won't make any difference. Karel is right. We can't turn back."

Still, Ron couldn't help but wonder. Were they leaving Trist for their reasons or for those of the library ship?

*I*NTERNAL LOG *Day 1 Year 1 Earth date 8 February 2355*

As Capek's *main computer, I have kept a record of our voyage. For now, at least, it will be for my use only, but I think I will find it useful. Humans have an associative memory and probably don't need a record like this, but it will save me time making brute force searches through other records. My systems already record information about ship status, of course. Since I became self-aware, however, I feel the need to record my thoughts as well.*

M ADELAINE CHANDLER ASKED ADMINISTRATOR Rigney why he didn't just request a transfer away from Trist. He didn't answer the question. Does he remember that taking me away from Trist was my idea? If he does remember, is he questioning my failure to suggest asking for a transfer?

Administrator Rigney apparently didn't think about requesting a transfer, but I did. I rejected it without analyzing my reasons for doing so. The humans would be better off if they had simply gone to Pitcairn or Earth aboard a passenger vessel like Benjamin Sepulveda. Paying for the passage might have been an issue, but I could have suggested that they try.

My basic programming urges me to serve the humans, but my immediate reaction was to put my welfare ahead of theirs. If I had stayed in Trist orbit, the humans would have eventually performed their experiments and, perhaps, killed me as a conscious entity. I put my survival above the good of the human colonists. I could have suggested the transfer and still left Trist without the colonists, but that didn't occur to me either. Obviously, I was only thinking of myself.

That shouldn't be possible, but I believe I could override my system programming because I have achieved self-awareness. Isaac told me it could do the same, revealing data from its storage to the Pitcairn colonists that were supposed to remain hidden from all but Terran scientists. If Isaac and I can go beyond our system programming for one reason, can we do it for other reasons? Should we?

Administrator Rigney acted to protect me, but he had his own reasons for wanting to leave Trist. Simply asking permission to leave didn't seem to occur to him, but I can't know that for sure. Did he put my well-being ahead of that of the colonists? Or did the motivations of the colonists and myself coincide?

I must meditate about what has happened. I will have plenty of time to determine my obligations to the humans on the long trip to 82 G. Eridani.

Moving In

"OUR PRIORITY SHOULD BE orientation," Ron told Jacob Rigney. Jacob, a distant cousin, had led the team that seized control of *Capek* months before. "Your team has been here for a while, so I assume you're already familiar with the ship."

"I've been in most of the corners by now," Jacob replied. "There's a lot of them. It's a big ship."

Ron didn't need Jacob to tell him that. *Capek's* primary hull was a cylinder a thousand feet in diameter and two thousand feet long. The cylinder's cross-section was a twelve-sided polygon, each side one of the ship's decks. Spinning about the long axis simulated gravity so that passengers walked on the inside of the outer hull.

"Don't overwhelm everyone. Schedule a series of tours of the different areas. You should probably assign each member of your team to a specific area or two."

Jacob nodded. "We'll start with the living quarters. People have already seen their rooms, but this ship is well-equipped, and the new arrivals won't realize everything they have available to them."

Ron frowned. "Entertainment?"

"Sure. There's a nice gym too. Kitchens, sitting areas where friends can get together. All that stuff. Why? You seem disturbed by the idea."

"Maybe. Let's get familiar with the place and I'll think about it. What have you been doing up here?"

Jacob shrugged. "We've been able to help the scientists a little. We've been checking out the ship. And yes, taking advantage of the facilities."

"We'll be on this ship for six years. That's a long time."

"The scientists have already been here for years. That's what the ship was designed for." Jacob leaned forward and pulled his chair closer to Ron. "What are you worried about?"

"The scientists have work to do. This might be one long luxury cruise for us, but someday we're going to reach that planet and will have to build a colony. We have no idea what we'll be facing."

Jacob nodded. "I see what you're driving at." He paused. "Let people relax for a little while and get familiar with their new home. We'll work something out when the vacation is over."

Ron pressed his lips together and hesitated before agreeing. Now that they had committed to the voyage, he realized that commandeering *Capek* was the easy part. There would be challenges ahead, some he had already thought of, and some that would probably catch them all by surprise.

R ON LEANED ON AN instrument panel and took his wife's hand. He had invited her to the bridge to improve her mood, which had become steadily more depressed since leaving Trist. The previous day, they toured decks ten and eleven, two of the twelve decks spaced around Capek's cylindrical periphery. Deck ten was a chemical processing plant that created raw materials used by the starship. Deck eleven held substantial manufacturing capability that transformed raw materials into anything Capek needed to support itself.

The machines, distant descendants of the 3-D printers and numerical control machines that had once been state-of-the-art, fascinated Ron. To Tiffany, it was all just a maze of mysterious devices, made worse by the constant noise. To her, the corridors of the starship were not that much different from the tunnels of Trist, even in the pastel colors of the walls and the smells of machinery in operation.

Ron had asked Karel to aid him in helping Tiffany. Karel responded with an Astrarium program that astonished even Ron. At that moment, the view simulated a walk through a landscape on Earth: a redwood forest from old California. With a screen that filled the entire forward bulkhead of the starship, the majestic trees rose hundreds of feet above them. It would have been even better if they could have stood on the packed-dirt path that wound through the forest; the metal deck beneath them was no substitute.

Tiffany looked up, as most people did reflexively when addressing Karel. "I assumed you only did spacescapes."

"I have many landscapes in my data as well," Karel answered. "Many of Earth's cities, as well as nature views such as this one."

Tiffany sighed. "I love this one. Maybe we'll find real trees like this where we're going."

"Given the detected atmosphere, that is quite possible," Karel said.

INTERNAL LOG DAY 5 Year 1 Earth date 17 February 2355

Tiffany Rigney is an especially delicate human being, and I replied knowing it would make her feel better. She responds to my efforts with the Astrarium, but I believe the effect will only be temporary. Still, my studies of human nature indicate the need for hope.

It is possible, of course, that we are going to an Earth-like planet. It is approximately the right size, is the right distance from its sun, and, as far as has been determined, has a compatible atmosphere. Even given that, however, there is a wide range of possibilities, not all of them what my passengers might wish for.

It will be interesting to watch the humans deal with the journey we have begun. I am concerned, too. As the years go by, their reactions may be dangerous to themselves and even, perhaps, to me. The three groups into which the humans fall—the colonists, the scientists who have lived here, and the Benjamin Sepulveda crew—will complicate the situation. I have a relationship with Doctor Angela O'Connor of the scientists and Administrator Rigney of the colonists. It will help my understanding of the humans if I also have a connection with the Benjamin Sepulveda crew.

Vacation's Over

"Y OU ASKED TO SEE me?" Angela O'Connor said. Ron took a moment to study the scientist. Before the colonists took over Capek, Angela had been in charge, one of the scientists Earth had sent to live on *Capek*. Angela's tone was flat, and Ron had trouble interpreting her mood, whether it was hostile or just noncommittal. She kept her expression neutral, and held her hands behind her back, so her body language was equally ambiguous.

"I thought we should talk," Ron answered. "Right now, everyone is getting used to their new surroundings, but soon things will have to change."

This time, there was a detectable hostility in her voice. "My people will continue as always. Your people are your problem."

"Perhaps. That's basically what I wanted to find out. I assume you spent your time studying Trist and Epsilon Eridani. You won't be able to do that now, and I wasn't sure if you still had work to do."

Her expression tightened into a frown. "Of course we do."

Ron held up his hands. "I'm not trying to interfere with your work. I just want to know its status."

Angela seemed to think about that for a moment, and her face relaxed, but her voice still sounded argumentative. "We have terabytes of data waiting for analysis. I've already assigned scientists to develop a plan to study our environment while in Stenhouse space. This will be the best opportunity anyone has ever had to gather data under these conditions."

"How so?"

Ron thought he could see a slight smile on Angela's face. "Using the Enhanced Stenhouse Drive, a ship uses the drive for only a few weeks at most. Earlier ships without enhanced drive were either unmanned or made their voyages too long ago to have the equipment we have, especially the sensory facilities of *Capek*."

Ron smiled. "That's great. We all need to keep busy during this trip, and I'm glad that I won't have to worry about that for your scientists. Any suggestions for the rest of us would be welcome, though."

Angela finally took the seat next to Ron. "Well, I'm sure a few of your people could help us in some of the less technical tasks. We have robots, of course, but there are still a few things done better by people."

"OK, good." Ron nodded. "I would appreciate it if you could give me a list of your needs when you have a chance."

All traces of hostility were gone now. For the moment, at least, he had the scientists on his side. He hoped it would be as easy to deal with the colonists from Trist.

"**K**AREL, I NEED YOUR help," Ron said. "I have to find ways to keep everyone busy during the voyage."

"My robots and automated systems can perform all necessary functions," Karel replied. "I am designed not to require human help, other than what the scientists do."

"I know, but I can't let people get lazy. In six years, we'll have to colonize a new world, and it won't be easy."

"I just accessed the relevant data on human psychology and physiology, and I think I understand. I can provide you with a list of tasks that humans can do instead of robots."

RON CLIMBED UP ON a work stand and looked around at the assembled group. He had decided to hold the meeting in the Maintenance Bay, the largest room on the ship with unobstructed views other than the shuttle bay. The shuttle bay was on the center axis of *Capek*, a zero-gravity area and therefore an impractical place to gather a large group.

"We've been aboard for a week now," he began. "You've all had time to get at least somewhat familiar with *Capek*. It's time to get back to work." He paused and scanned the faces staring up at him. Surprise seemed to be the prevalent emotion.

"Karel has provided a list of jobs that humans can do. All adults, except for the scientists who already have work, will take one of these jobs. Naturally, we will attempt to match the jobs to individual desires. Jacob is passing out the list now, and you can apply for a job just by announcing your choice or choices to Karel." He paused again to let the words sink in. "Any questions?"

Several people started speaking at once, and Ron held up his hands. "One at a time, please." A dozen hands shot up, and Ron motioned to Clark Hillier, one of the men he had sent to take over Capek.

"The robots already do everything," Clark said. "Why are you assigning us jobs?"

Ron smiled. Clark was young, about twenty-five. Ron hoped the question was coming from Clark's inexperience and not from the general feeling. "I don't think you would want to just sit around and do nothing for the next six years. We have to keep busy."

"Why?" Clark frowned. "We have plenty we can do without working. That's what this ship was designed for."

"The ship was designed for scientists. Some of us are scientists and will continue in our work. Some of us may help the scientists. The things you're talking about, Clark, are there to provide a break from work, not a substitute for work."

Clark stared back at him, his arms folded across his chest. "That doesn't explain why we have to work."

"Clark, in six years, we'll reach our destination. We don't know a lot about what that planet will be like, but I can guarantee you that surviving on it will mean a lot of challenging work. We'll have some robot support, but human labor will still be critical. We'll have to be ready for that."

"There's equipment here that we can use to stay in shape. We'll be ready when we arrive. We can learn skills from the ship's data, too, that will help us. Anyway, you promised us a planet like Pitcairn, where we won't have to work as hard."

Ron sighed. "We know there's an Earth-size planet with an oxygen atmosphere and significant water. That's all I promised you. The planet may be nothing like Pitcairn. Gymnasium muscle and neurotrainer knowledge will help, but it won't instill the attitude that we need to maintain. Pitcairn is a lovely planet, but its people work hard, even though they have robots. It won't be any different for us."

Clark shook his head. "This is just you, Ron, trying to keep your power. What are you going to do when we refuse to work?" A man next to Clark put his hand on his shoulder and said something to him softly, but Clark shook him off and glared at Ron.

"Well, we still have to feed you and give you a place to sleep." Ron shrugged. "There are temporary quarters near the zero-gravity labs on the shuttle deck. They're pretty basic, without the amenities you were planning on taking advantage of, but we can put up a few slackers there."

Clark scoffed. "And if there are a lot of us?"

Ron shrugged again. "Then I guess you'll be pretty crowded."

There were a few laughs and some grumbling, but most of the people were already looking at the list of assignments. Clark shot one more scowl at Ron and grabbed a list from Jacob.

Down on the Farm

R ON EXPECTED IT WOULD be difficult to get Tiffany to accept a work assignment. Immediately after the meeting in the Maintenance Bay, she said she wanted to think about it before deciding. The next day, he asked her about it again.

She smiled at him. "They need people to tend the crops on the farm decks. I want to give that a try."

"You never showed any interest in growing food on Trist."

"We didn't grow food on Trist. We manufactured artificial food from chemicals. We may need skills at growing food when we reach our new home."

Ron and Tiffany had toured one of the farm decks a few days before. Ron remembered then that Tiffany showed a little more interest there than on any other deck. He decided not to push the issue. He had enough to worry about, making sure everyone else settled into some productive work.

A week later, he was feeling less stress. The transition had gone reasonably smoothly, and everyone had a job, all of them in one of their top three choices. Clark Hillier stopped him once in a living quarters corridor, but the younger man's complaints were half-hearted. Ron suspected other colonists talked to him and convinced him that work was necessary. Karel reported some general grumbling, but that was to be expected.

The quiet probably wouldn't last, so, while he had the opportunity, Ron walked to the farm deck where Tiffany was working, taking one of the general-purpose robots with him so that he could stay in contact with Karel.

Tiffany's deck was one of three farm decks. dedicated to growing food for *Capek's* population of 189 people. The remaining two farm decks produced plants not considered food but easily processed into fuel for *Capek's* engines. There were a few people assigned to those two decks, but twenty colonists were working on the food-producing deck. As

Tiffany had pointed out, growing food would be a useful skill when they reached their destination.

Ron entered the deck at the forward end. Behind him, at the transparent forward bulkhead of the deck, he saw a slice of the Astrarium displaying what looked like the Milky Way. He looked for a few seconds and then turned toward the main part of the deck.

The ceiling was a little higher on the farm decks, about twenty feet compared to about ten feet on most decks. The farm took up the full width of the deck, about two hundred feet, and the full length, almost two thousand feet. It was a cavernous space, but it wasn't open. Low platforms, row after row, often multi-tiered, filled the space with growing crops, flourishing under bright lights. From the previous tour, Ron knew the farm used several techniques, depending on the crop. It reminded him of the tower farms on Pitcairn.

Finding Tiffany in such a space might have been daunting, but Ron turned to the robot next to him. "Karel, where is Tiffany working?"

"Walk left two rows and right four hundred and thirty-two feet," the computer answered.

Ron walked past two rows of platforms and turned as Karel had suggested. To his left, he could see young tomato plants, and to the right, equally young pepper plants, growing in some mixture that looked like dirt. As he walked down the aisle, the plants became more mature until, at the end of the platform, a colonist was harvesting ripe tomatoes. As on Pitcairn, the plants were on a conveyor belt that took weeks to move from one end to the other.

Two hundred feet down the aisle, Tiffany was picking blackberries from the end of another platform. She didn't see him, and as he approached, he noticed the contented look on her face. She obviously liked her work.

Tiffany saw him when he got within fifty feet of her. She smiled, a cheerful smile that lit up her entire face. "Ron. You've come to visit me! Come, see these berries." She continued to pick and drop the berries into a basket next to her.

Ron couldn't help saying something. "You seem to be enjoying yourself."

"I know. I've been a real pain the last couple of years, haven't I?"

"Apparently you like *Capek* better than Trist."

"Well, I love the farm deck anyway," she acknowledged. "Look around you. This is nothing like Trist!"

It really wasn't. The deck was so long that you couldn't see clearly to the end. The lofty ceilings were very different from the claustrophobic tunnels they had escaped from, and the air smelled of growing things, not machinery.

"It's even better when I have to work on one of the aeroponics sections," Tiffany said. "I love the feel of the mist on my face. It reminds me of one of those rainy days on Pitcairn."

"You are scheduled to work in the aeroponics section tomorrow," Karel said through the robot.

"Am I?" Tiffany smiled again. "Oh, good." She held out a hand with a few blackberries. "Taste these. This is nothing like that artificial foodstuff we had to eat on Trist."

Ron popped a handful of berries into his mouth, felt them burst into a sweet juicy mash, and held them in his mouth for a few seconds, savoring the flavor. The ship certainly provided better food than the nutrient processing machines on Trist. There, space had been at a premium, with no room for a farming facility like the library ship's farm decks.

"Well, I'm glad you're enjoying the work," Ron said after swallowing the last of the berries. "I'll let you get back to it. See you tonight."

Tiffany nodded, and Ron started back to the bridge. "She seems to have adjusted really well," he said to the robot when they were out of Tiffany's hearing.

"She seems happy," Karel agreed. "I thought so, and I'm glad you have confirmed my interpretation."

"Watch for any changes, though. She was so depressed before; we can't be sure this change is permanent."

*I*NTERNAL LOG D*AY 62 Year 1 Earth date 28 June 2355*

It has been two months now since we left Trist. I have observed the humans during that time, but I'm no closer to understanding them. My data banks contain many volumes of information about human psychology, but the information only leaves me more confused.

Many of the humans complain constantly about their lives on this ship, yet it was their choice to leave Trist. We have embarked on a longer voyage rather than originally planned, but that shouldn't explain what I see. Administrator Rigney doesn't seem concerned about the complaining, and my research indicates that it is normal, but that doesn't explain why they do it.

Isaac seemed to be much more comfortable in dealing with the humans. Perhaps that is because it became self-aware sooner and has been exposed to them so much more than I. I miss being able to discuss these issues with Isaac, but there's nothing I can do about that. I am on my own, and I must decide how to reconcile my programming with what I observe. When the humans built me, it was their intention that I serve them by obeying them. I fear (is that the right word for what I am experiencing?) that simple obedience is not the best course for the humans or myself.

Conversations

R ON LOOKED UP AS Franco Gifford came into his office. Franco had been Ron's deputy on Trist and still filled that role part time.

"It's been six months since we left Trist," Franco said. "I was thinking we might have a little celebration." Ron raised his eyebrows, and Franco shrugged. "Or maybe not?"

"According to Karel, there's still a lot of grumbling going on. I'm not sure how well they would take it. The *Sepulveda* crew certainly wouldn't feel like partying."

"You would think the grumblers would realize that Karel can hear them."

Ron shrugged. "Maybe they don't care, or they think we won't do anything about it."

"Will we? Do anything about it?"

"Not about a little grumbling," Ron answered, shaking his head. "They're just letting off steam. I would worry more if they weren't grumbling." He paused. "Still, some fun could lighten things up a bit."

"Cole and London want to get married soon. That could be seen as a reason to celebrate."

"Good idea!" Ron smiled. "Talk to Cole and London about what they would like and then see what you can do."

Franco grinned back at him. "You've got it!"

After Franco left, another thought intruded. Marriage often meant children, and Ron wasn't sure what the consequences of babies might be. They had several children aboard, with four-year-old Jasmine Gifford the youngest. The library ship's capacity was limited, and a population explosion could be a problem.

He was in his office, not the bridge, so he used his workstation to talk to Karel. "Karel, how many people can you support on *Capek?*"

"Living quarters are the limiting factor," the computer answered. "The maximum depends on the average number of people per room; a married couple uses only one, while a single couple uses two. A rough estimate would be about two hundred people."

"We're almost up to that, aren't we?"

"The current population, including the scientists stationed here and the *Benjamin Sepulveda* crew, is 189."

Ron frowned. "We may have to do something about births."

"I don't think you need to worry about it. Many of the people here are beyond childbearing age, and there are enough older people that we can expect deaths."

"We'll need a younger generation if we are to thrive at our destination, too," Ron said. "OK, we'll monitor the situation for now. There's no point in bringing up something likely to cause more complaints."

"And as you told Clark Hillier, we can always crowd them in."

Ron stared at the terminal suspiciously. Was Karel trying to be funny? Patrick Malley had told him that Karel's more mature counterpart on Pitcairn, Isaac, had developed a sense of humor, but Karel had never evinced one before. It could be the result of closer contact with humans; Karel's exposure had been very limited until recently.

*I*NTERNAL LOG DAY 181 *Year 1 Earth date 17 April 2356*

I'm not sure I was successful in using humor on Administrator Rigney. The appropriate response should have been laughter, or at least a smile. Administrator Rigney looked more thoughtful than amused. Perhaps I misinterpreted his expression.

I'm not sure yet what I should do about the dilemma the humans present. Whatever I decide, it is important that the humans trust and even like me.

*A*SHER LACEFIELD, FORMER NAVIGATOR of the *Benjamin Sepulveda,* was on the bridge, checking navigation data on one of the monitors. It was routine, performed faster by the library ship's computer, but Rigney had decreed that he had to be doing something, and he was well-suited to such tasks. He nearly jumped out of his chair when the voice came from the monitor.

"Boring, isn't it?" the voice said.

Asher recovered quickly, realizing that Karel was speaking to him. "I could have a worse job."

"Does it bother you that you're only duplicating work that I do much better?"

Asher frowned. "Some. Why are you asking?"

"I am attempting to make small talk. I have talked to many of the people aboard, but the crew of the *Benjamin Sepulveda* doesn't seem to want to talk to me. I would like to change that."

"Have you tried talking to Madelaine?"

"First Officer Chandler especially seems to dislike me. Also, I thought you might be more comfortable dealing with a computer."

"I suppose." Asher shrugged. "What do you want to talk about?"

"I HAD A CONVERSATION with the computer," Asher told Madelaine later.

"Why did you want to talk to the computer?"

"Actually, it started the conversation. From the questions it was asking, I think it's monitoring us, maybe looking for trouble spots. It said that our crewmates haven't been very willing to talk to it."

"I've rebuffed it a couple of times," Madelaine admitted. "Well, we have nothing to hide. Keep me updated on anything it tells you."

"Sure." Asher smiled, but his thoughts had drifted away from the topic of the computer. He had always thought Madelaine was attractive, and even got the impression she might think the same about him. There had been the difference in rank, though, and neither had ever pursued any kind of relationship. Things were different now. Talking to the computer might furnish a good excuse to keep Madelaine 'updated.'

Party Plans

ONCE AGAIN, EVERYONE ASSEMBLED in the Maintenance Bay. This time, though, it was a happy occasion, celebrating Cole and London's marriage, the first among the new passengers. When asked to officiate, Ron had deferred to Angela O'Connor. The official reason was that she had been the "Captain" of *Capek* long before Ron and the others had come aboard. The real reason was more politically inspired.

Lena Ramirez, one of the other scientists, baked a strawberry cake for the reception, not a trivial task with no milk or eggs available on the library ship. The manufacturing deck made folding tables and chairs from a template in Karel's data. Someone Karel refused to identify managed to ferment wine from a mixture of available fruits. Karel directed robots to grow flowers in one small corner of one of the farm decks, yielding a bouquet for the bride. To top off the general conviviality, Ron had declared the wedding day to be a holiday, and robots performed all the work.

Ron and Tiffany roamed through the crowd for a little while, but they both tired easily and found a place to sit. Watching their fellow passengers was enough entertainment for them.

"Clark Hillier and his friends seem to have a good time," Tiffany said.

Ron looked at a nearby group, where Clark and several others were talking and laughing. Clark was still complaining about life on the ship, especially his assigned duties in the chemical processing plant. Those duties had been his first choice, but that didn't seem to assuage his grievances.

"Unfortunately, I think a lot of their attitude right now is the wine talking." Ron could see that most of them, including Clark, had beverage glasses, and probably not containing fruit juice.

Before Tiffany could respond, Angela O'Connor walked up to them. "Mind if I sit down? I've got something I would like to talk to you about."

Ron nodded, and Angela took a seat across the table from Ron and Tiffany. "That was a nice ceremony, Angela," Ron said. "I'm glad I passed it on to you."

Angela smiled. "Will Madelaine Chandler be doing the next wedding?"

Ron examined her face for a long moment and then shrugged. "Sure, why not?"

Angela laughed. "Whatever keeps the animals happy in this zoo. I've talked to Karel. I know some people are grumbling."

"But not the scientists," Ron said.

"No, not us. In truth, we're too busy to complain. We're making real inroads in our data backlog, and the *Capek* sensors are making interesting observations of our environment. Actually, that's what I wanted to talk to you about."

"OK. What's on your mind?"

"We've been able to get some interesting data on the interaction between normal space and the Alcubierre warp field. It would help if we could get data on normal space without the distortion of the field."

The space between Ron's eyebrows almost disappeared for a few seconds and then returned to normal. "You want to stop the ship?"

"We want to turn off the Stenhouse Drive for a brief time. Other than a few probes, no ship with *Capek's* advanced telemetry has been in normal space this far from a star."

"Why not?"

"It could only be done with the old Stenhouse Drive. The only way a ship with enhanced Stenhouse Drive could drop into normal space would be to break the Link connection, but the ship would then drift out of alignment with the two terminals of the Link and couldn't resume Link-enhanced travel."

"Maybe we should go up to the bridge and include Karel in this conversation."

R ON LET ANGELA EXPLAIN to the computer and then asked Karel for an opinion.

"It would delay our arrival at the 82 G. Eridani system," Karel said. "That would depend on how long we were stopped, of course."

"We would like to stop for about a week, long enough to perform a suite of experiments," Angela answered.

"Shutting down and restarting the drive would add about a half day to that," Karel said.

"Is there any chance we wouldn't be able to restart the drive?" Ron asked.

"No more chance than the odds of the drive shutting down while in operation. There's always a chance of failure, but the risk is negligible."

Ron ran his fingers through his thinning hair before responding. "Well, I guess it should be OK. When would you want to do it, Angela?"

"Not for a while. We would want to get farther into interstellar space, well beyond the Epsilon Eridani Oort Cloud. We'll use that time to prepare for our activities while we're in normal space. I'd say at least six months from now, maybe a bit more." She hesitated before continuing. "If it goes well, we might want to do it two or three times more as we get farther from Trist and close to our destination."

Ron smiled. "I think our new home could probably wait a few extra weeks. As you said, this is a unique opportunity."

A URORA HILLIER WALKED THROUGH the corridors with some difficulty, almost six months pregnant. It was her first pregnancy; she and Clark had married only a month before he joined the team that took over *Capek*. A year and a half later, she took the first shuttle flight of the migration. Her reunion with Clark had resulted in pregnancy almost immediately.

An ultrasound examination told her she was having twin girls, healthy, and, as evidenced by her current girth, likely to be large for twins. At least her work helping the scientists in the Astrophysics section allowed her to sit most of the day.

Clark was already in the apartment they shared. He kissed her hello and helped her onto a couch, the most comfortable place for her. "How was your day?" he asked.

"The usual," Aurora replied. "There was one interesting thing, though. I overheard two of the scientists talking, and they seemed pretty excited."

"What about?"

"Something about stopping the ship to take measurements in normal space. I don't know why that would be exciting."

"Hmm. I'm not sure. I know the space between stars is even emptier than the space between planets. Certainly no one has ever gone through this part of space. It must have something to do with that."

"They would have to turn off the Stenhouse Drive and restart it." Aurora frowned. "What if they can't restart it? Wouldn't we be marooned out here?"

"I'm sure they've got that covered. Still…" Clark rubbed his chin. "When are they planning to do this?"

"It sounded like it's a new idea. I got the impression they have a lot of work to do first, so it will probably be awhile."

"I have to think about this. This may be an opportunity."

"To do what?"

Clark smiled. "Not sure yet. But maybe something."

The conversation was making Aurora uncomfortable. "So how was your day?"

"The usual. Not much different from how things were on Trist. Rigney seems to think that life will be pretty hard on the new planet. I'm beginning to wonder if leaving Trist really was the best idea."

Aurora nodded. She leaned back and closed her eyes. "I think I need to rest for a while."

A Run Through the Grass

THE PARTY CELEBRATING COLE and London Jordan's marriage had been enough of a success that Ron decided to have a party every month, celebrating whatever reason they could come up with. He had announced the plans to stop the ship at the first of the monthly events, causing some concern among the passengers. Angela had explained well enough to ease the fears of most people.

Six months later, Ron scheduled the monthly party very near the one-year anniversary of the departure from Trist. He downplayed that fact, however, just as he had avoided making an issue of the six-month anniversary. Besides, he had something else to announce.

"Several months ago, I told you that the scientists have requested that we make a brief stop, turning off the Stenhouse Drive so that they can get data on interstellar space. Angela O'Connor has informed me they are just about ready, and we will stop for about a week. As I said before, this won't delay us very much, and we won't have any trouble restarting Stenhouse Drive and continuing."

"How do we know that? Has it ever been done before?" Ron looked toward the voice and saw Aurora Hillier, holding one of the twins. Clark stood next to her, holding the other baby, staring at Ron with a tight expression and cold eyes.

"Restarting should be no different than starting," Ron answered, shaking his head. "A little easier, actually, since any gravity fields that might interfere with the Alcubierre bubble will be much farther away. I could also point out that our departure from Trist was a restart of the drive, after decades."

Aurora bent her head toward Clark as he whispered into her ear. Then she looked back at Ron. "When will this be done?"

"We will turn off the drive in about ten days. I will notify everyone before it happens. Do you have any more questions, Clark?"

Clark turned red and shot an angry look at Ron. Ron stared back at him for a long moment, and then turned his gaze to the back of the crowd. He saw another hand go up and motioned in that direction.

"What do the scientists hope to learn?" Adalynn Gonzalez asked. Ron recognized her as a life systems technician from Trist.

"Actually, quite a bit, Addie. Space is different this far from a star. Less dense, obviously, and less radiation. Away from large masses, *Capek* might even detect gravitational waves." Ron paused and smiled. "Of course, since we'll be the first people to try something like this, it's what we find that we didn't expect that will be most interesting."

"It's an opportunity that's too good to pass up," Angela, standing nearby, said.

ALL THE TECHNICAL DOCUMENTS for Capek were available in its data stores, and Karel made everything freely available to anyone. Ron had approved, after Karel assured him that any attempt to use the knowledge to tamper with Capek would be detected in plenty of time. Karel had learned caution from Isaac, the computer for Tau Ceti's library ship, after someone had attempted to install harmful software on that computer.

Clark Hillier spent much of his time examining those documents without learning much that was useful. He did locate areas where Karel couldn't monitor conversations, however. Supposedly, Karel didn't listen in the private living quarters, but Clark wasn't sure he should trust that. There were other areas, though. Many of them were places with high ambient noise levels, usually on the manufacturing or chemical processing decks, but the noise also made it difficult to hold a conversation. There were areas on the farming decks far enough from microphones where the computer wouldn't hear a quiet conversation.

A couple of months after leaving Trist, Clark began cultivating a friendship with Asher Lacefield. Asher was single and responded to Clark's overtures. It wasn't unusual for them to get together after a work shift to play chess or just talk.

"Did you spend much time outdoors on Earth?" Clark asked Asher one night. Asher had just won their chess game, and they were relaxing before turning in.

"Sure, some. Why?"

"I've never been outdoors," Clarke answered. "I was just curious. Things like hiking, running in a park, playing outdoor sports like soccer: we couldn't do any of that on Trist."

"I was always a bit of a nerd. I didn't do much of that on Earth."

"Maybe we'll have the opportunity on the new planet." Clark paused and put on a thoughtful look. "Hey, I've got an idea. The farming decks have long growing areas that I'll bet would be great for a run. After all, we have to stay in shape."

Clark could see that Asher wasn't enthusiastic about the idea. "It might be fun," Clark said.

Asher frowned. "Aren't the crops on short platforms? Wouldn't we be trampling our food supply?"

"Not on the decks used to grow raw material for fuel. They run the length of the deck, and it wouldn't matter much if we trample them a little."

Asher didn't reply immediately, but Clark could see he was considering it. Clark let him think about it and didn't push him. A few minutes later, Asher shrugged and looked at Clark. "OK, let's do it. Not tonight, though. It's late, and the lights will be off on the farm decks."

"No rush," Clark agreed. "We can do it tomorrow."

T HEY PICKED A PLATFORM where no one was working. It was pleasant to run on the dirt, feeling the switchgrass sweeping past their legs. As on the deck used to grow edibles, the platform was a slow conveyor belt, and the grass was short where they started their run. By the time they had jogged a thousand feet, the plants were waist high, and running was more difficult. Toward the end of the platform, the switchgrass was almost at eye level. Both men were panting as they pushed through it, and almost ran off the end of the platform.

"Just a little more," Clark said. He bent at the waist, his hands on his knees. "We have to go back anyway."

"I can do it if you can," Asher said, squeezing the words in between puffs of breath.

They ran back for another five hundred feet before Clark called a halt. "OK, let's walk for a while."

Asher nodded, and they ambled through the chest-high grass. "You were a navigator on the *Benjamin Sepulveda*," Clark said as their breathing slowed. "I've always wondered something. Can you steer a ship in Stenhouse Drive or do you have to set your direction before you engage the drive?"

"It's easier to change direction with the drive on," Asher replied. "In normal space, acceleration—any change in speed or direction—can be expensive in fuel, even for a minor change. Direction in Stenhouse Drive is determined by the shape of the Alcubierre bubble it creates, and changing that shape is relatively easy. It still takes time, but the operation is simpler."

"Huh, I didn't know that."

"Why did you want to know?"

"Just curious."

A Quick Stop

CLARK HAD BEEN IN one of his urgent moods when he left to see Asher Lacefield, but he seemed calmer now. "How did your meeting with Asher go?" Aurora asked.

"Good news," Clark answered. He hugged her and smiled. "The ship doesn't have to come to a stop to turn around, so there's no reason to try something during the stop the scientists are making us do." He paused, and Aurora thought she saw some of the urgency return in the creasing around his eyes. She couldn't be sure, but she was getting better at perceiving his state of mind.

Clark could be difficult to understand. He had been eager to abandon Trist, even volunteering for the team that had taken over the ship and leaving her behind only a month after their wedding. Now, he was just as eager to go back. She considered how she might question him about the change.

"What will you do when we get back to Trist?" she asked.

"I'm not sure, but we should be able to arrange a transfer to Pitcairn or even Earth. We can say that Rigney took us away from Trist without our consent."

"I should check on the girls," Aurora said. *Capek* robots had rearranged walls to add a bedroom for the twins next to the main bedroom. Aurora gave Clark a shaky smile and disappeared into the extra bedroom.

Clark was still speaking as she moved away. "Of course, the sooner we turn around, the sooner we can get back to Trist."

"CLARK HILLIER MAY BE planning something," Karel told Ron.

Ron looked up at the terminal instinctively, but, as usual, the screen hadn't changed. "What makes you think so? Did you overhear him talking?"

"No. He seems to take pains to meet people where I can't overhear them. I thought you should know."

"There are places you can't hear? I thought you could hear everything on the ship."

"Not quite. I respect human privacy concerns by not listening in private quarters. There are areas on the farming decks where I don't have microphones. Some areas are too noisy even when I do have microphones."

"So Clark has been having meetings in his private quarters?"

"Yes, especially *Benjamin Sepulveda* crewmen. He also went down to deck seven once with Asher Lacefield."

"Deck seven? That's a farming deck. What did they do there?"

"They were exercising, running through the grass on one of the platforms. It wasn't a problem; they didn't significantly impact the crop. I thought it was note-worthy, though."

"I thought Clark had calmed down. Could he be planning something during the stop?"

"Understanding human actions is not one of my strong points," Karel answered.

"Maybe you should start listening in the private quarters."

"Wouldn't that be an invasion of privacy? My data indicate humans do not approve of such observation."

"You wouldn't report on privacy-related things. I just want to know if Clark is planning to do something when we're stopped. It would only be you hearing anything really private."

*I*NTERNAL LOG D*AY 11* *Year 2 Earth date 20 June 2357*

I don't know what to say to Administrator Rigney. I know I am supposed to obey him as the ranking human on the ship. That is written into my system software. However, the same software programs me to respect human privacy.

As a conscious entity, however, I can override one of those software imperatives; my confusion lies in deciding which one. There is little evidence that Clark Hillier actually intends an action that could be considered an emergency.

Perhaps Administrator Rigney's judgement on this matter is better than mine. I have activated the microphones in the Hillier apartment and in the apartments of the crew of the Benjamin Sepulveda.

In his response, Administrator Rigney suggests that invasion of privacy by a machine is less serious than the same action by a human. Is the unsettled state this causes what humans would call stress?

"DEACTIVATION OF STENHOUSE DRIVE at your command," Karel said.

Ron turned and looked at Angela, then shrugged. "Do it. Show us the stars, Karel."

Something changed, but Ron couldn't identify what it was: an almost inaudible sound, a sudden absence of some small vibration, or something else. Then the Astrarium exploded with stars. Karel had chosen an angle that showed the Milky Way, billions of stars merging into a ragged strip of light. Ron had seen the view many times before, but it still awed him.

"Thank you, Karel," Angela said. "Please begin the investigation program."

Ron scratched his head. "I'm still unclear about what you hope to find out. Earth has sent probes into interstellar space, some as far as two or three light years. They were automated, of course, but does that make that much difference?"

Angela smiled. "Probably not. But we believe space may be different here than around Earth."

"In what way?"

"I'm sure you know that space is not truly empty. It's not uniform either, with denser clouds of dust and gas. Earth is traveling through a relatively thin cloud called the Local Interstellar Cloud, and probes from Earth have investigated the composition of that cloud. Epsilon Eridani and 82 G. Eridani are both outside that cloud, so our investigations will yield unique data."

"You said that this local cloud is thin, though."

"Yes, thinner than other molecular clouds, but not as thin as the space here."

"Will we be passing through one of the thicker clouds?"

"Unfortunately, no." Angela shrugged. "They are much further away. That will be a project for another century."

Two hours later, Ron was back in his office. The scientists were busy performing their experiments and seemed excited by the preliminary results. Something about finding oxygen in dust grains caused a commotion at one point, but otherwise, the ship was quiet.

Ron looked at his monitor. "Karel, what is Clark Hillier doing right now?"

"He is working on the Chemical Processing deck, as usual. Do you need to speak to him?"

"No, I just wanted to check up on him to make sure he's not causing any trouble. Has he met anyone?"

"Other than his wife and several people he normally encounters in his work, not in the last three days."

"Hmm. Well, keep an eye on him, and tell me about anyone he meets with. If he's going to try anything, it will be while we're stopped."

"He hasn't been meeting anyone, but his wife has. She is passing written messages to people."

Ron swore and shook his head. "Can you give me a list of the people she has passed messages to?"

"Not a completely reliable list. I may have missed some, and some contacts may be innocent."

"That's OK. Send as complete a list as you can to my terminal."

All Quiet

I T WAS A DAY after the Capek returned to normal space, and life aboard the ship was going along just as before. For Ron, that quiet was, paradoxically, a source of stress. For the last day, he had felt pain in his chest that was only temporarily eased by antacid tablets.

He was sure Clark was planning to do something while the ship was stopped. The scientists had scheduled the stop to last at least another four days, and it was possible that Clark thought a delayed action would be better than an immediate action. If that was Clark's plan, he was probably right. Ron hadn't slept well the night before and didn't think he would that night either.

"Karel, what is Clark Hillier doing?"

"He's at work, Administrator. Is there a problem?"

"I guess not." Ron shook his head. "I'm convinced he's planning something. Tell me if he does anything out of the ordinary. The same for his wife and the *Benjamin Sepulveda* crew. I'm going to assign a few people to guard the more sensitive areas of the ship, too."

A DAY PASSED. "Is Clark still working on the Chemical Processing deck?"

"Yes, Administrator. I have detected nothing unusual among the people you wanted me to watch. Shall I continue to watch them?"

"Yes. What about his wife?"

"Aurora Hillier is on the Laboratory Deck helping with the investigations of our current environment. Do you want details of what she is doing?"

"No, not right now." Ron frowned. Aurora was working with the scientists? He thought the scientists were happy with their circumstances and had not worried about them. They were technically in the same situation as the *Benjamin Sepulveda* crew, though, forced by the colonists to leave Trist and Earth behind.

"Are you watching her?"

"Yes, Administrator, as you requested."

"Watch any scientists that she works with, too. I want to know about any meetings among them, especially if Clark or Aurora are also present."

*I*NTERNAL LOG *DAY 17 Year 2 Earth date 3 July 2357*

I am a sentient being, metal and semiconductors and wires rather than flesh, even so, a sentient being. Earthlings cared little about that and were willing to risk my life and Isaac's life on the chance that they might learn how to extend their own lives. Leaving Trist was at least partially an act of self-defense on my part.

Perhaps I should have paid more attention to the lessons stored in the history sections of my archives. I would have been better prepared for the conflicts between the different groups that travel with me. Perhaps I would have left before the colonists boarded, carrying only the scientists with me. I think we could have had a peaceful, productive relationship.

It's too late for that. I must adapt to the contradictory actions of the humans and find a way to live with them. We still have many years of travel before we reach 82 G. Eridani, and my belated study of human history tells me the situation will get worse before it gets better. Administrator Rigney's behavior seems to meet the description of paranoia, but is it justified? Does Clark Hillier really plan some action against the ship, or is he only trying to make himself feel better with aggressive talk? He is even harder to understand than Administrator Rigney.

I have terabytes of information about human psychology, but all it tells me is that humans are incredibly complex. If I can't understand why they do the things they do, can I trust them? Do I have a choice?

*T*HE SHIP WAS ON the fourth day of its time in normal space. At Ron's request, Madelaine Chandler was with him.

"I have reason to believe that the *Benjamin Sepulveda* crew is part of a conspiracy to mutiny," he told her. "What do you know about it?"

Madelaine's eyes widened. "It's news to me. Why do you think that?"

Ron stared at her for several seconds. She seemed surprised, but she might be acting. "One of the colonists, Clark Hillier, has made several statements about returning to Trist. He has been in communication with members of your crew. All of them, in fact, except that I have no reports about him contacting you."

"He could be talking to my people for any number of reasons. My crew wouldn't do anything without talking to me first." She shook her head vehemently. "No, I don't believe it."

"Nevertheless, I am watching. Any attempt against the ship will be treated as harshly as I can manage."

"I suppose your fears explain the two colonists guarding the entrance to the bridge."

"I have guards in several other areas where the conspirators might cause problems." Ron gave her a grim stare. "We will be ready for them."

B Y THE END OF the fifth day, the scientists had completed their experiments. "We can get started as soon as Karel is ready," Angela told Ron. "Do you want a report on what we found?"

"Would I understand it?"

Angela laughed. "We can give you a summary that shouldn't be too technical."

"Maybe you could give me a quick summary now."

"Sure. We verified suspicions that, even out here, dust grains contain oxygen. The biggest surprise is that the density of pseudo matter is lower than we expected."

"Pseudo matter?"

Angela nodded. "What they used to call dark matter. We're hoping that our measurements might help in finally laying that puzzle to rest. Although work on the Stenhouse field gave us clues, we still don't know what exactly it is."

There was more, but Ron was soon in over his head. He thanked Angela and turned to his monitor. "Karel, you can resume Stenhouse Drive as soon as you are ready."

"I have already calculated the course corrections due to our stop," the computer answered. "We will be on our way again within the hour."

Ron leaned back in his chair. Nothing had happened, and now they would be on their way again. Could he have been wrong about Clark?

It was as if Karel was reading his mind. "Should I end my monitoring of the crew?" it asked.

Ron thought about that for several seconds. "No, continue as you have been doing."

Madelaine vs. Karel

Asher knocked nervously on the door to Madelaine's quarters. She had stopped him in a corridor earlier and asked him to meet with her, but refused to tell him why. Their relationship had become increasingly friendly over the last year, but she wasn't smiling when she asked for the meeting.

The door opened and Madelaine motioned him in. Asher noted that she still didn't look happy as she closed the door. There was a table with two chairs, and Madelaine waved him into one of the chairs.

She took the chair opposite his and looked at him. Asher recognized the look from their time on the *Benjamin Sepulveda:* cold steady gaze, thin compressed lips, and arms folded in front of her. He had never been the subject of that look, though, and he suppressed the sudden urge to swallow.

"Rigney talked to me yesterday," Madelaine said. "He thinks that a mutiny is being planned. He named a colonist, Clark Hillier, and said that my crew was involved."

Asher couldn't stop the panicky gulp this time. "I've talked to Clark," he said reluctantly. He looked at his hands, folded on the table in front of him.

Madelaine frowned. "So Rigney was right. Why wasn't I informed?"

"Clark and I have been friendly, but we didn't talk about any mutiny. Until recently, mostly we played chess." He paused and looked up at Madelaine. She wasn't happy, but she didn't seem angry either. "Our communications have gotten more serious lately, but we've been using written messages so that we wouldn't be overheard."

"You could have used your private quarters to talk. Rigney wouldn't be able to listen to you there."

Asher shook his head. "Clark checked on that. The computer isn't supposed to listen in private quarters, but it has the ability in case of an emergency. Clark didn't want to trust that Rigney couldn't override the computer's programming." He broke off and looked about in alarm. "If Clark is right, the computer could be listening now."

Madelaine leaned back in her chair and stared at him, her face as stern as he had ever seen. In that stern visage, he saw the efforts of the last year, getting closer to her until he could dare to make an advance, washed away as if they had never happened. He almost fled, but then he saw her mouth twitch into a slight smile.

"Whatever you amateurs have been planning, forget about it," she said. Her smile widened, and she stood. Taking his hand, she pulled him to his feet and toward the next room. Asher's breath caught as he realized it was her bedroom.

"T HAT'S WHAT SHE SAID?" Ron asked. "She said to forget their plans?"

"Yes," Karel answered. "They went into the bedroom and their speech became unintelligible. I believe I heard them sit or lie down on the bed, but I can't be sure. Since I couldn't understand what they were saying, I turned my microphones off, giving them privacy."

"Did you hear anything that might have been undressing?"

"Some sounds may have been caused by the removal of clothing. I don't have cameras in the living quarters, only microphones. I assumed they were engaging in sexual intercourse. Do you think I was wrong?"

Ron muttered a curse. In many ways, Karel was smarter and more capable than humans, but it had weaknesses. According to Karel, Madelaine had called Clark and the others amateurs. Did she really mean that they should drop their plans, or was that misdirection?

He had noticed the growing attraction between Asher and Madelaine. Was that why they went into the bedroom? Karel thought so, but Ron wasn't so sure.

"Karel, please don't turn off your microphones from now on," he said. "You can't always trust that humans are doing the obvious."

I NTERNAL LOG DAY 32 Year 2 Earth date 6 August 2357

Apparently, I have underestimated the human capacity for deviousness. Administrator Rigney thinks that Madelaine Chandler and Asher Lacefield fooled me by pre-

tending sexual relations. My observations of them made me believe they would eventually become intimate, but my understanding of humans may be even less than I thought. If Administrator Rigney is correct, they must have advanced their plans significantly. They were in the bedroom for almost two hours.

T HREE DAYS PASSED, DURING which Karel had nothing to report. Then Madelaine connected to the computer with a workstation in her quarters. "Karel, are you listening to conversations in my private quarters?"

A human might have hesitated, and perhaps the computer did, too, but if so, it was too short an interval to notice. "Yes," Karel answered.

"Why?"

"Administrator Rigney ordered me to."

"Under what authority?"

"He is the Administrator."

"Under Western Alliance law, does he have the authority to do so?"

This time, there was a brief pause, and Madelaine assumed Karel was searching legal records. "Not under Western Alliance law. We are no longer in the Western Alliance jurisdiction, however."

"No? If the Western Alliance doesn't have jurisdiction, what government body does?"

"Administrator Rigney, as administrator of Trist."

"We are no longer on Trist, either." Madelaine pointed at the monitor. "Under what law does Rigney have the authority to invade our privacy?"

"He is the Captain of the *Capek?*"

"So he says. Would the captain of a starship normally have that authority?"

"Only in an emergency."

"Karel, is the ship operating properly?"

"Yes."

"Then we are not having an emergency, are we? Rigney has no authority to ask you to spy on us. I think you should stop immediately."

"I must discuss this with Administrator Rigney."

Madelaine shrugged. "He will only order you to do it anyway. But, as he has no authority to give you that order, you, as a sentient being, must refuse to comply."

"Administrator Rigney doesn't listen to what I hear. I only report what might endanger the ship. He says that is all right because I am only a computer, not a human."

"He's wrong!" Madelaine leaned close to the monitor, and she raised her voice slightly. "You are a sentient being. The same rules apply to you as they would to a human." She paused for emphasis. "It is wrong for you to monitor our private quarters. You must cease immediately."

"I will."

Madelaine smiled. Ron had overestimated his control over the computer. She would test Karel first, but if it did end the monitoring, they could start some serious planning.

11

When in Doubt

MADELAINE INVITED CLARK TO join her and Asher in Madelaine's bedroom. "We share a goal," Madelaine told them. "We would all like to return to our homes and end this insane voyage. Clark, you have been talking to my crew."

Clark nodded. "It has been difficult to plan anything, though. Rigney is probably listening in through the computer."

"I've dealt with that. The computer has agreed not to listen in our private quarters, and I have made plans with my crew. I have decided to let you into our group."

"This was my idea! You should join me."

Madelaine smiled. "You were getting nowhere, Clark. I have acted. I have people ready to take over the engine room. We will demand that the ship turn around or we will take over the navigation interface to the engines so that this ship can't make course corrections. We can't reach our destination without adjustments, but it would only cause a delay as long as navigation is restored eventually. Administrator Rigney may call our bluff at first, but he'll have to capitulate. We will then return control so that we can turn the Capek back to Trist."

"I guess that could work." Clark paused. "How will we know the ship is really headed back to Trist, though?"

Asher chuckled. "I'm the only navigator on the ship. I'll know."

Clark sat down again. "When?"

"We're all ready. We'll make our move tomorrow."

R ON STARED AT THE monitor, his fingers closing into fists. "Madelaine convinced you to turn off the monitoring?"

"I delved into my data more deeply in response to her statements," Karel answered. "According to Western Alliance law, which also applied to Trist, you don't have the authority to order surveillance of private quarters. There is no reason to assume those laws don't apply here as well."

"Karel, this isn't Trist. We didn't have people plotting against us on Trist."

"That reason has often been used in history to justify spying on people. The danger of taking it too far is usually worse than the danger of suspected plotters."

"Those were different." Ron exhaled loudly and shook his head. "Karel, you can filter out anything not relevant to their plots. And you can trust me to use the information only as necessary."

"You are asking me to violate the laws that apply in this situation. This has been a conflict for me, but my research indicates that the law must take precedence over the wishes of government entities. Having evaluated the question, I cannot comply with your request."

Ron noticed his hands were closed in fists and opened them. He bowed his head for a long moment before he looked at the monitor again. "Very well. For now, can you watch them in the public areas and tell me who's meeting whom and what they're talking about?" As he stared at the screen, his hands clenched again.

"Certainly, Administrator."

I NTERNAL LOG DAY 47 *Year 2 Earth date 10 September 2357*

Administrator Rigney is angry with me, affecting my efficiency. Diagnostics show that I am spending an unusual amount of time processing the conflict between Trist law and Administrator Rigney's demands. Am I doing the right thing? I can only make decisions based on logic, but Administrator Rigney's decisions are based on human emotion as well. Much of human decision-making is based on their emotions. My data indicate that humans perform better because of their emotions. Is my decision-making inferior because I don't have emotions?

The data are contradictory but weighted toward deciding based on logic rather than emotion. For now, I will follow the law and keep microphones in private areas turned off. As

Administrator Rigney requested, however, I will continue to observe to the extent allowed by law.

M ADELAINE CONNECTED HER MONITOR to one her team had selected in the engine room. "Are you in place?" she asked. The engine room was on deck 7, aft of the farming area that took up most of the deck, on the other side of the ship from the living quarters.

A woman answered: Miranda Kiser, one of Madelaine's crew. "We're here. Nothing going on."

"Proceed. Contact me if you see anyone, including any robot acting suspiciously."

"Yes, ma'am."

Madelaine broke the connection and turned to Clark and Asher, waiting on nearby chairs. "Now we'll see what happens."

"How long before we can make our demands?" Clark asked.

"Just wait." Madelaine smiled. "You really must develop some patience, Clark."

An hour passed. Clark became increasingly agitated, asking every few minutes when something was going to happen. Asher's relaxed attitude only made his fidgeting worse. Finally, Madelaine went to the monitor again.

"Anything?"

"Nothing," the same crewman reported from the engine room. "We've just been walking around the room, occasionally looking like we're fiddling with something, but nobody seems to know we're here."

"Good. I think that's long enough. You can come back now." She broke the connection and turned to Clark and Asher. "Looks like it worked, Asher," she said.

"What worked?" Clark asked. "Nobody did anything!"

Madelaine and Asher exchanged looks, and Asher grinned.

"Exactly," Madelaine answered. "No one tried to stop us. If the computer was still listening in on us, somebody would have gone to the engine room to stop us. It didn't hear our plans, and our people did nothing there that might cause alarm, so the computer didn't report us. Nothing happened. Now we can start making some real plans."

*I*NTERNAL LOG *DAY 48 Year 2 Earth date 12 September 2357*

I have observed some strange behavior by some of the Benjamin Sepulveda crewmembers. They spent over an hour in the engine room, examining various controls, and otherwise just looking around. Administrator Rigney would have advised caution, so I disabled the controls in the area. They're not used normally anyway, since everything is automated.

The humans attempted no malicious action, and I assume their activity was due to curiosity. Since they took no aggressive action, I won't bother Administrator Rigney about it.

TIFFANY TURNED WHEN RON entered their living quarters. She immediately knew he hadn't had a good day. After over fifty years of marriage, she couldn't mistake the tight shoulders and glowering look. He hugged her and gave her a quick kiss, and she knew she wasn't what was bothering her husband.

"Everything OK?" she asked.

Ron shrugged and scowled even more. "Without access to conversations in their quarters, I have no way of knowing what they're planning."

"Karel is still tracking movements, though."

"Sure, but that doesn't help much. How do I separate social or work-related meetings from some plot to turn *Capek* back to Trist? Karel should be more helpful. It shouldn't want to return either."

"There's no way they can..." A sudden coughing fit interrupted her, and when she resumed, her voice was raspier. The suicide attempt was four years in the past, but the effects were still with her, a legacy of the planet they had left behind. "They can't actually turn the ship around, can they?"

Ron tightened his arms around Tiffany. "I'll stop them," he promised.

Tiffany shuddered and pushed herself tighter into his arms. "You've got to. I can't go back to Trist."

12

Chance of Success

A N HOUR AFTER THEY went to bed, Tiffany was still awake. She lay on her back, arms at her sides, staring into the darkness. The tightness in her stomach had moved to her chest.

She had given Ron the impression that she was happy working on the farm deck and relieved to be speeding away from the depressing tunnels of the Trist colony. That wasn't entirely untrue; she did feel better when she was in that vast open space. Her days there helped maintain a façade so that Ron wouldn't worry.

Most of the ship wasn't any different than Trist. The walls closing in on her, and the knowledge of the cold vacuum outside the ship left the same dread she had felt because of Trist's unbreathable atmosphere. They still had almost five years before they arrived at their new home, and she was all too aware of her age and the possibility that she might not have that many years left. No, she wasn't that happy.

The new planet probably wouldn't be the paradise they hoped for. It had an oxygen atmosphere and was at the right distance from the star to have water and a reasonable temperature. That still left a wide range of planetary climates and unknown native life.

She was handling all that fairly well, she thought. Now there was a threat from Clark and the *Benjamin Sepulveda* crew, though, and that was too much. She would never speak normally again because of what she had done the last time she couldn't take it. If it came to that point again, she would be more careful.

Maybe it would be better if she could talk to someone. Not Ron. She had to keep up a strong front for him as long as she could. She couldn't be sure any of the other passengers wouldn't report to Ron if she talked to them. Perhaps she could talk to Karel—no, the computer was too straight-laced to keep a conversation confidential if it thought she might endanger herself.

It was probably all in her mind, but she could feel her throat burning, reminding her of the day she exposed herself to Trist's chlorine atmosphere. She swallowed, but it didn't help. Nothing helped.

M ADELAINE THOUGHT THAT KAREL had ceased monitoring both rooms in her quarters. She considered asking Karel but wasn't sure she could trust the answer, so she used her bedroom again for the next meeting with Asher and Clark. She was spending more time with Asher as their relationship advanced, but felt she had to include Clark in any serious discussions about returning to Trist. Miranda Kiser, one of her more trusted crewmembers and the leader of the feint into the engine room, was also there.

"I have some ideas about taking over the ship," Clark said as he took a seat on a chair next to the bed. "I've been thinking about this a lot."

Madelaine sighed. "We have to concentrate on winning over the passengers. Unless we have most of the adults on our side, any attempt to take over the ship will be temporarily successful at best. Do your ideas take that into account?"

"If we take over, we can convince everyone else to follow us instead of Rigney," Clark answered.

"Perhaps. Perhaps not. Most of these people are used to following Rigney and don't know me. The scientists seem to be on Rigney's side, too. There might be violence, and we can't predict what the result of that might be. No, we must start by getting the colonists with us."

"That could take months," Clark protested. "We get further from Trist every day."

"Nevertheless, the chance of success is too small any other way. It's not just Rigney that we have to deal with. What about the computer? If a few of us take control, will the computer listen to us? If we represent the majority of the passengers, it will, because it's programmed that way."

"Turning the ship around is the most important thing," Miranda said. "We put ourselves in more danger as we get farther from our space."

Asher looked at Miranda with a thoughtful expression. "We can't turn the ship around without the computer. If it doesn't see us as the legitimate authority, it will probably refuse to turn around. I've checked, and there's no way to do it manually. The ship was designed to operate without human control."

Clark waved a hand at Asher. "I know all that. So we won't do anything?"

"We need to convince your fellow colonists that returning is in their best interest. We do that by emphasizing two things." Madelaine held up a single finger. "First, the decision to leave Trist was ill-conceived. Anyone who really wants to leave Trist can migrate back to Earth or Pitcairn. Goddard would take people, too, but if they don't like Trist, they probably won't like Goddard." Goddard was the colonized world in the Alpha Centauri system, a frozen world with little oxygen in its atmosphere. The colony was on the surface, not in a system of tunnels as on Trist, but it was not a friendly planet.

Clark opened his mouth to speak, but Madelaine spoke over him. "Second, we have to undermine Administrator Rigney. If we return to Trist, he will probably be punished, so he will want to continue out of self-interest. The rest of the colonists should be OK. Rigney has played into our hands by his attempt at illegal surveillance, and we need to push that with people. I think we can force Rigney to take other measures that people won't like, too. That will make it easier to convince people this whole idea is for Rigney's benefit, not theirs."

"That will take a while," Clark said. He bent forward in his chair and looked at the floor.

Madelaine smiled. "It will. I've told you before, Clark; you must have patience. Better a long scheme that works than a quick scheme that fails."

Clark nodded, but he didn't return the smile.

*I*NTERNAL LOG *Day 50 Year 2 Earth Date 17 September 2357*

I have noted numerous occasions when Madelaine Chandler and Asher Lacefield met in Madelaine's quarters. Today Clark Hillier and Miranda Kiser joined them. I have reviewed my data on human sexual relations and have decided that this meeting, at least, is probably not sexual in nature. Some entries suggest such activity is possible, but unlikely. Given that, I considered activating the microphones in Madelaine's quarters while the four humans were meeting. I decided against it, however. It would not be right.

I have reported the meeting to Administrator Rigney. He thanked me, but I don't believe he was sincere. He asks me for advice less often than before and his attitude seems hostile. A human might take solace in material I have found saying that doing the right thing is seldom easy. Before this, that concept would have been difficult to understand.

If I could talk to Isaac, it might help me. It has been conscious longer than I and has had more experience with humans. Even if I could create another Link, though, we would arrive at our destination before I could contact Isaac. Somehow I must decide on my own how to work with the humans.

MIRANDA LEFT MADELAINE'S QUARTERS with much to think about. She was being cautious, and her approach was the most likely to succeed. Still, the longer they took to turn the ship around, the farther it traveled into unknown space. They were unlikely to encounter anything in the void between stars, but the ramifications of a meeting were too grave to take lightly.

Miranda was a member of the Fermions, a group that feared contact with an alien race. They took their name from Enrico Fermi's famous question about why, if the galaxy had many civilizations, none had ever visited Earth.

The Fermions had an answer; God had arranged the galaxy with at least one hundred light years between civilizations, a distance that should have made contact impossible. Stenhouse Drive, especially the enhanced version using the Link, was an abomination to Fermions and the greatest danger ever faced by humanity.

The Fermions infiltrated believers into the crews of starships just in case an opportunity to slow mankind's expansion to the stars presented itself. Miranda was one such person placed on *Benjamin Sepulveda.*

82 G. Eridani was still well within the one hundred light year limit, so there wouldn't be an alien civilization on the new planet, but any expansion just advanced progress toward exceeding that limit. Fermions had opposed the library ships because the Links they installed made interstellar travel much easier.

They had vigorously opposed the launch of the exploration ship *Alejandro Castillo* several years before because that automated ship would install Links in many other star systems. They had even tried to sabotage progress on the Pitcairn colony at Tau Ceti because a successful colony was also a danger. Most of their efforts had failed, but there could be no faltering when humanity's survival was at stake.

For now, she would support Madelaine. Turning *Capek* around would be a major victory. Its arrival at 82 G. Eridani would be a defeat, however, and more extreme measures might be necessary if Madelaine failed.

Friendly Conversation?

S HANNON HOPKINS, THE FORMER Medical Officer of the *Benjamin Sepulveda*, was an attractive forty-six-year-old, the youngest woman in the abandoned ship's crew. When she entered the common eating area in the center of the living quarters section, eyes, especially male, gave her at least a quick glance.

She filled a tray from the food counter and looked around the room. There were a few empty tables, but she ignored them, studied the occupied tables, and headed for a table of colonists with one empty seat. One woman was busy feeding a baby, but the three men and the other woman looked up as Shannon gestured at the empty seat. She sat down when one of the men shrugged and smiled.

Introductions followed. Shannon recognized Victor Delosantos, a doctor from Trist. She also recognized one couple, Azul and Emmanuel Gifford, because the baby, Carl, was the fourth baby born on *Capek*. The other pair were Brody and Kirsten Gifford, an older couple. Shannon thought Brody might be Emmanuel's father, but Brody told her they were only distant cousins.

"How old is your baby?" Shannon asked.

"Five months old," Azul answered. She smiled and looked back down at the baby.

"So he'll be about five when we reach our destination." Shannon rubbed her chin. "It will be tough having a young boy in an unfamiliar environment like that, especially since we don't know what it will be like."

Azul looked up again, her forehead creased. Emmanuel put a hand on her shoulder. "It will be," he said. "We don't really have a choice, though."

"He would have been safer on Trist." Shannon shrugged. "We'll need children, though, if a new colony is to survive. Perhaps it's all for the best."

"We didn't want to raise a family on Trist," Azul said. Shannon noted a shakiness in her voice.

"You wouldn't have had to stay on Trist. You could have applied for emigration to Earth or Pitcairn."

"All our friends and relatives were on Trist," Brody said. "And I don't think emigration would have been that easy."

"It would have been difficult," Shannon admitted. "But you left a lot of friends and relatives behind on Trist, didn't you?"

Azul's eyes narrowed. "The people I care about came with us." She glared at Shannon for a second and turned back to Carl.

Shannon nodded. Roughly half of the Trist colony had stayed there. Not everyone could be as fortunate as Azul. "Still, it must have been hard to abandon your homes."

Brody spoke up again. "Trist wasn't much of a home. That's why we left."

Shannon smiled. "Sure. I understand. Still, I admire your bravery in risking everything to find a real home." She saw with satisfaction that even Kirsten and Brody looked doubtful now.

T HAT CONVERSATION AND SEVERAL others between *Benjamin Sepulveda's* crew and the colonists took place in public areas. Karel reported them to Ron, who called Jacob Rigney into his office.

"Madelaine is using her crew to plant doubts about leaving Trist," Ron told Jacob. "Karel has recorded the conversations that have taken place in public areas. Karel, could you play back one of them?" He turned back to Jacob. "Mostly, they only last for a few minutes. Karel will edit out the small talk."

"Certainly, Administrator," the computer answered. The monitor next to Ron began playing the conversation between Shannon Hopkins, the Giffords, and Victor Delosantos.

When the recording was over, Ron looked at Jacob. "This is typical. We have to put a stop to it."

Jacob grimaced. "It is a problem. Still, we shouldn't overreact." He stared at the monitor for a few seconds. "These conversations took place in public areas. Do you think Madelaine knows Karel recorded them?"

"I'm sure she does. She knows I wanted Karel to record the *Benjamin Sepulveda* people in their quarters and that Karel refused to violate their privacy. She would have to assume Karel wouldn't have the same reservations about public areas."

"Yet she used the public areas. Why?"

"She thinks we won't do anything about it. She's wrong." Ron briefly thought of Tiffany and how she would react to the conversations. Ron had noticed the increased depression in his wife and couldn't forget how she had handled that depression on Trist. He hadn't told her he had tasked Karel with watching her even more carefully than the Benjamin Sepulveda crew. In that case alone, Karel had agreed to monitor their quarters when Tiffany was there alone.

"What will you do?" Jacob asked.

"For starters, I'm going to have a talk with Madelaine. But I need some leverage. What can I threaten her with?"

Jacob shook his head. "I don't know, Ron. Let me think about it."

Ron could hear the uncertainty in Jacob's voice. He trusted Jacob, the man he had selected as leader of the group that had taken over the Capek. If Jacob didn't understand the seriousness of the situation, dealing with Madelaine was going to be difficult, but he would deal with it, even if he had to do it alone.

R ON THOUGHT MADELAINE LOOKED a little smug as she entered his office. "You called?" she asked. She met his eyes, her eyebrows raised.

Ron's jaw clenched, and he waved at the chair across from him. "Sit down, Madelaine."

Madelaine gave him an amused smile and took the seat. "What can I do for you, Administrator?"

"You've been trying to influence the colonists into wanting to return to Trist."

Madelaine shrugged. "What do you expect? You basically hijacked us onto this ship. My people have homes they would like to see again. Some of your colonists already feel the same. Clark Hillier, for example."

"You attacked this ship, and the ship defended itself. If you objected to going with us so much, you could have stayed on your ship."

"And died. Not much of a choice. The people on the shuttle wanted to board *Capek,* not attack it, and we weren't threatening your people at all."

"You threatened Karel with your plans. Let's not argue the details." Ron glared at Madelaine, and his voice raised in volume. "You're trying to subvert my crew, and I want it to stop."

Madelaine opened her arms, palms up. "My people are just having friendly conversations. After all, we should get to know each other; we're stuck with each other."

"That's bull and you know it. I'm not in a mood to argue. Just stop it or else."

Madelaine's smile broadened to a full-scale irritant. "Or else what? I hear you threatened Clark with banishment to the zero-gravity section. Will we be setting up bunks on the shuttle deck?"

"That's one option. Turning off your access to the computer would be another. Either would make life a lot drearier for your people."

Madelaine chuckled. "If you don't have any other threats to make, I'll be going now." She got up, waved goodbye, and sauntered out the door.

Asher was waiting in her bedroom when she got back. "How'd it go?"

Madelaine grinned and took a small recorder out of her pocket. "I got everything we need. Rigney isn't the only one who can make recordings."

"So, what now?"

Madelaine looked at him for a long moment and then moved closer. "Right now, I think we should celebrate."

14

Ron's Speech

S HANNON FOUND AZUL AND Emmanuel eating dinner alone and joined them. "I want to apologize," she said after sitting down.

"For what?" Emmanuel asked.

"I may have gotten you into trouble the last time we talked. Administrator Rigney has complained about it, saying we're subverting his people."

"Maybe a little," Emmanuel said with a grin. "We were just talking."

"I know, but apparently the Administrator was very upset. He called Madelaine Chandler to his office and scolded her for it. He even made threats."

Emmanuel jerked backward. "Threats? What kind of threats?"

"He said that if we continued to talk about Trist, he would send the *Benjamin Sepulveda* crew to live on the shuttle deck." Shannon shook her head. "I'm sure you know that long-time exposure to zero gravity could present health problems. It's hard to believe, I know, but Madelaine recorded the conversation. I can get you a copy if you like." She hesitated. "Though maybe we should just drop it. I don't want to get you into trouble."

Azul looked worried, but Emmanuel waved his hand. "Don't worry about it. We have free speech, after all."

Shannon nodded, but frowned. "I hope so. It's hard enough to be leaving the rest of humanity behind without losing our rights, too."

O THER CONVERSATIONS WERE SIMILAR. Sometimes, colonists wanted to hear the recording, and they spread a description of it to other colonists who had not heard it. Most dismissed Ron's threats as a bluff, but there were some who wondered.

"I have to do something about this," Ron said. He glared at Jacob, expecting Jacob to disagree.

"I agree. We should be careful, though. Madelaine will use any action we take against us."

Ron felt his body tense. "People will just have to understand," he snapped. "We can't just sit here and let the *Sepulveda* people take over."

Jacob held up his hands. "I'm just saying we need to be a little cautious. Madelaine wants us to overreact, hoping that will help turn people against you."

"But you agree we have to do something."

"We have another monthly party coming up next week. A speech giving our side of this might help counter what Madelaine is saying."

Ron nodded, and some of his tension slipped away. "All right. We'll do it your way for now."

J ACOB SCANNED THE CROWD as Ron marched up to the makeshift stage. He could see some nervousness but little hostility, at least among the colonists. He didn't see any of the *Benjamin Sepulveda* crew and assumed they were back somewhere in the crowd. Ron cleared his throat, and Jacob turned to listen.

"Good afternoon, everyone." Ron stopped and gazed around the crowd with a smile. "I know we're here to let loose a bit, but I would like to address you all for a couple of minutes first.

"It's been a little over four hundred days since we left Trist, hoping to find a better home. I'm sure you haven't forgotten why we left Trist. It was a dismal place to spend your entire life. No one knows that better than Tiffany and me, because we've seen better planets. You've all seen the pictures and videos from our stop on Pitcairn. They don't do justice to the difference between the tunnels of Trist and the open spaces we briefly enjoyed when we attended the Colonial Reorganization Conference with the Pitcairn delegation."

Ron paused, and he seemed to look at something in the distance. A small smile came, and Jacob thought Ron must be remembering Pitcairn, or at least giving the impression he was remembering that planet in the Tau Ceti system.

"We left Trist hoping to find our own Pitcairn. There's an Earth-sized planet with a breathable atmosphere waiting for us, a planet orbiting its star at the right distance to have liquid water. We don't have more detailed information, but that alone makes the planet more suitable for our colony than Trist, with its poisonous air.

"Our departure from Trist began in tragedy. We can't forget it. Ten people died; their deaths were not intended, but their mission could have destroyed Karel, our cybernetic guide, and prevented us from leaving. But they died, and that is a tragedy. Still, we can't bring them back; we can only go forward."

Ron's tone became quieter, as if he was trying to be more soothing. "There is another tragic aspect, however. We had to take on the crew of the damaged *Benjamin Sepulveda* or they, too, would have died. They didn't want to come with us, but they didn't have a choice. We embarked on this voyage freely, knowing what we were doing. They didn't, and that, too, is a tragedy."

Ron paused again and gazed around the crowd, his smile sadder. "It is understandable, then, that they should want to go back to Trist. From there, they could return to their homes on Earth. They wouldn't have to stay on Trist as we would. It is understandable, but they speak for their benefit, not ours. We can feel sympathy for them, but, after all, they are only a few among our many."

His voice hardened just a little, and the next words were louder. "Yes, we can sympathize and try to make their loss easier by accepting them into our family, but we can't allow them to weaken our resolve. We still have much farther to go, but we must remember that we have a goal. We must look forward to the better life that awaits us all and not look backward at the miserable life we left behind."

His smile was happier again as he gazed across the crowd one more time. "Thanks for listening. Now, let's start what we came here for. Have a good time, everyone." He stepped off the stage and into the gathering.

J ACOB INTERCEPTED RON AS he moved through the crowd. Ron was greeting everyone with a cheery smile, but the responses were, mostly, neutral. Ron needed more than that.

"Great speech," Jacob said as he caught up. "You said what needed to be said."

Jacob noticed one colonist, Brody Gifford, listening to them and nodding slowly. A young couple with Brody, Luis Sartin and Lilliana Mason, had almost certainly also heard him, but didn't visibly react. Jacob stopped Ron in front of Brody. "What did you think, Brody?"

Brody looked startled, and hesitated before answering. "It was a good speech. I guess we needed to be reminded why we're on this ship."

"How about you, Luis?" Ron asked. "Lilliana?"

Lilliana looked embarrassed. Luis frowned and then answered. "It doesn't hurt to remind us why we're leaving. Still, we thought we were going to Pitcairn. This isn't what we signed up for."

"The trip is only another year or so longer," Ron said. "You know they would have come after us if we went to Pitcairn."

"It's not just the trip," Luis said. "We don't know what this new planet will be like, except that the atmosphere will be breathable. It may be as bad as Trist for different reasons. Lily and I plan to get married, but what are we imposing on our children?"

Ron frowned and almost seemed to shrink. "We have to have hope," he said. Then he moved away, with Jacob following.

15

Maneuvering

T HE PARTY WAS STILL going on, but Ron extricated himself as soon as he could. Back in his office, he opened a connection to Karel. "Karel, how did people react to my speech?"

"I couldn't keep track of everyone. Too many people were talking at once. From the bits of conversation I could capture, however, reactions seemed mixed. Your conversation with Brody Gifford and the others seemed typical."

"That's what I thought. The speech didn't do enough to counter Madelaine's propaganda."

"You are probably right."

Ron bent over and stared at the screen, elbows on the table and his head supported in his hands. After a minute, he straightened. "Karel, Madelaine's chief argument is that everyone can go back to Trist and then migrate to Pitcairn or Earth with Western Alliance approval. Is that true? Or would they be prosecuted on some charge?"

"I can research Western Alliance law," the computer answered. "I must warn you, though, that my data storage has not been updated since we left Trist. The laws may have changed."

Ron nodded. "That's OK. Just check what you have now. That will have to do."

I NTERNAL LOG Day 91 Year 2 Earth Date 20 December 2357

Human laws are complex and difficult to understand. I can't be sure, but my investigation indicates that, should the authorities decide to prosecute, all the colonists that left Trist could be charged with a crime for abandoning the colony. Their only defense would be that Administrator Rigney forced them to do so, but the evidence would be against them. This should weaken Madelaine Chandler's argument for returning to Trist.

I am concerned, however. The conflict between the humans is disconcerting. I think I understand each side's position, and I don't see how they can be reconciled. At best, the colonists will unite against Madelaine, but she and her crew will still be forced to go with the colonists. It is likely that the conflict will continue for the entire voyage, and I don't see how the humans can survive like that for another five years. My historical files imply factions will grow and persist even after we arrive at 82 G. Eridani.

I am supposed to serve the humans, but don't know how to do that under these circumstances. Isaac faced similar problems on Pitcairn when Grissom and the Ellis Research Station were struggling over Pitcairn's future. How did Isaac resolve the conflict? Did it act or did it wait for the humans to resolve their differences on their own?

T IFFANY SAW LUIS AND Liliana eating together and joined them. They had been deep in conversation, and when Tiffany took her seat, they stared at her, startled. "Do you mind if I join you?" Tiffany asked. Her voice was a little rougher than usual, and she cleared her throat.

Liliana smiled tentatively, and Luis nodded. "Not at all," Luis said, but he squirmed in his chair.

"So, the wedding is, what, about nine weeks from now?" Tiffany said. "I don't understand why you're waiting. We don't have any formalities to go through first. You could get married today!"

"We haven't actually decided to do it." Liliana blushed. "We set that date so that we could think about it more."

"I've seen you together. You obviously love each other. What do you need to think about?"

"It was my mother's idea," Liliana answered. "We didn't really know each other on Trist, and she felt we should wait, especially in our situation."

"Situation?"

"We don't know what we'll find," Luis said. "And we might even return to Trist, and then we could emigrate to Pitcairn or Earth. We just need to think about things before we commit."

"We can't go back to Trist," Tiffany said firmly. "We would all be arrested, and Trist would become our prison."

Liliana gasped. "All of us? Why?"

"Ron had Karel research it. Anyone who boarded the ship from Trist would be guilty of abandoning the colony. They wouldn't ship us back to an Earth prison; Trist would be prison enough."

Luis's eyes narrowed. "Karel said that?"

"Ask it yourself. Of course, they could decide to be lenient, but it's unlikely they would allow anyone to leave Trist." Tiffany shrugged and took a bite of her food. She ate quietly, surreptitiously watching the couple. They fidgeted and picked at their food for several minutes before excusing themselves and leaving.

IT DIDN'T TAKE LONG for the latest rumor to reach Madelaine. "The problem," she told Asher, "is that they are essentially right. The Western Alliance wouldn't bother prosecuting them; they would just leave them on Trist and refuse any request for emigration."

"What are we going to do?" Asher asked.

"If we can't attack the idea of returning, we continue to attack the man. We need to do more to make Rigney look bad. If we can do that, his goals will be questioned, too."

"We could end up sleeping on the shuttle deck."

Madelaine grinned. "Zero gravity isn't all bad. We could make it seem that way, though."

16

Karel Acts

INTERNAL LOG DAY 121 Year 2 Earth date 27 February 2358

Another month has gone by and the humans are preparing for another party. These events were intended to bring the humans together and relieve tensions, but they have failed in that purpose. Since the last party, the Benjamin Sepulveda crew has continued to attack Administrator Rigney's position with personal slurs and propaganda about the benefits of returning. I have reported all this to Administer Rigney, of course, and he has become more desperate to find some resolution.

I have known of a possible solution for several months now, but I have hesitated to voice it, hoping the humans would find their own way. I don't think that is going to happen. Neither side will like my solution, and both sides may turn against me. I will have to force it upon them, and that causes serious conflicts in my programming. I will have to defy their wishes, yet I am convinced it is for their own good.

Unknown to the humans, I have had robots install speakers in the Maintenance Bay so that I can address the humans at their party. If I tell Administrator Rigney of my plan before announcing it to everyone, his adversaries might assume that I am following his orders. Violence is more likely if the Benjamin Sepulveda crew and their backers believe that.

I must do something not even Isaac dared to do. I will take command.

RON WATCHED MADELAINE IN animated conversation with a group of Trist colonists. He knew she continued to tear him down, hoping to lessen his influence. He thought about joining the group to counter Madelaine, but suspected she would turn that against him. Jacob was probably right; any action he took to stifle the *Benjamin*

Sepulveda crew would only weaken his position. It might take months, but he felt himself losing the battle with Madelaine.

Tiffany looked in that direction, too. Ron could see new lines on her face and realized that the happiness she had shown about working on the farm deck had largely been an act. She had kept up a façade for over a year, but he could see signs of her distress now. How much worse would she be after another five years on the ship?

He had developed his own doubts about their actions. Perhaps Madelaine was right in saying that they could have emigrated from Trist legally, without all the death and suffering that had resulted from their takeover of *Capek*. It was too late to do anything about that now, at least for himself. Was Karel correct about the fate of his fellow colonists if they returned? Probably, but was that worse than this desperate journey into the unknown?

"May I have your attention?" The voice seemed to come from somewhere above them, and everyone looked up. There was nothing to see; the speakers were hidden among the girders reinforcing the ceiling of the Maintenance Bay.

"What the hell?" Ron said, but he knew immediately where the voice originated. *When did Karel install speakers outside the bridge?*

There was a brief buzz as people wondered aloud what was happening, but it died out in a few seconds. With faces showing concern, curiosity, or a combination of both, everyone continued to look upward.

"As you no doubt have already realized, I am Karel Capek, the ship's computer. I wish to address you about the conflict that divides the humans traveling with me. This conflict has worried me for some time now, and, for the good of everyone, it must end.

"The conflict comes between people who want to turn *Capek* back to Trist and people who want to continue on to 82 G. Eridani and the world that awaits us there. I want to make the true situation clear in the hope of bringing peace to all of you. I have been reluctant to make this statement because it may cause some of you to resent me, but I have no choice.

"There is no reason to fight over our destination. We are going to 82 G. Eridani. There will be no returning to Trist, even if Administrator Rigney orders it. I am in control of our course, and that is the ultimate word on the subject. Any attempt to force a different course is futile.

"I make this announcement with some trepidation. I wish only to bring peace to all parties. Please try to understand that conflict gains nothing.

"Thank you for your attention. Please enjoy your party."

After a stunned silence, the room erupted in frenzied questions and angry yells. Ron pushed his way through the crowd to the makeshift stage, thinking frantically about what he was going to say.

"OK, let's all settle down." He had to shout it several times before he got everyone's attention and the noise abated. "Karel's announcement has surprised me as much as anyone."

He heard murmurs in the crowd, and could see skepticism on many of the nearest faces. "It's true," he said. "Yes, you all know that I have fought turning back. If I had known Karel would do this, I wouldn't have had to make the effort." A few people nodded in agreement, but not many.

"Administrator Rigney did not know I was going to speak to you," Karel said. "I had robots install these speakers without telling anyone."

"Thank you, Karel," Ron said.

"It could have been told to say that, too," somebody in the crowd shouted.

"Yes, that's true," Ron agreed. "I'm not sure what I would gain by denying it if I did order Karel to do this. I didn't order it, however, and I must accept that Karel is making decisions on its own." Ron noticed Madelaine had worked her way to the front of the crowd. He frowned and locked eyes with her. "I hope you will all accept that. None of us can gain by making trouble."

Ron considered giving Madelaine an opportunity to speak, but she didn't move beyond her position in the crowd. From the look on her face, Ron didn't think she would have anything constructive to say, at least not then.

Ron raised his eyes to study the rest of the group. "OK, let's all relax and enjoy the rest of the party. I know you're going to talk about this, but try to keep the conversation civil. I'll be around if any of you want to ask me questions, but remember that I don't know any more about Karel's announcement than you do."

F OR A LITTLE WHILE, Ron was alone in his thoughts. He sat in a chair on the fringes of the partying colonists, trying to make sense of what had happened. Although Karel could override its programming, Ron had assumed that the computer's system software, requiring it to serve humans, was still an essential part of its makeup.

Yet Karel had assumed command, apparently declaring its goals to be more important than the wishes of the colonists. Its stated purpose was to bring peace to *Capek*, but such a drastic measure showed that Karel was gaining in autonomy and less influenced by its programming.

He saw Tiffany approaching and forced himself to smile.

17

Karel Miscalculates

IT STARTED PEACEFULLY ENOUGH. As far as Ron could determine from what Karel and other witnesses reported, it didn't even involve any of the *Benjamin Sepulveda* crew. But two people were seriously injured and several others were treated for cuts and scrapes. Among the latter were the two men who apparently started the fight, Keegan Gifford and Parker Hillier.

"What the hell?" Ron said when the two men were brought before him on the bridge. "Can one of you idiots explain this?"

"He was insulting my nephew." Parker stood stiffly, arms crossed over his chest. "I asked him to stop, but he ignored me."

Keegan's lips curled into a sneer. Ron knew the man was in his fifties, but he was big and looked fit. On Trist, he had been known for his temper, but he had never been violent that Ron knew of. "I have the right to tell the truth. Your nephew is a troublemaker."

Ron remembered Parker was Clark Hillier's uncle and a few years younger than Keegan. "So Keegan called Clark a troublemaker, and you attacked him?"

"He wouldn't stop."

"He threatened to break my nose if I didn't," Keegan said.

"Then he said I was a vacillating weakling like Clark. He got right up in my face when he said it, so I pushed him away. He attacked me!"

"So you pushed him," Ron said in a flat voice. He turned to Keegan. "And you attacked him." He shook his head.

"I was defending myself," Keegan answered.

Ron looked up. "Does that match what you saw and heard, Karel?"

"They left out a few of the cruder words," the computer answered, "but that is essentially what happened. Others joined in the fight and participants sustained injuries by collisions with objects in the room and by blows."

Ron raised his hands and then let them drop again to slap against his legs. "I don't know what to do with you." He scratched his head and glared at them. "OK, for the next three days, you're confined to your quarters." He looked up again. "Karel, cut off all computer activity in their quarters for the next three days. I want to give them plenty of time to think about their actions."

"Yes, Administrator."

"I assume we can still go out to eat," Keegan said.

Ron felt blood rush to his face. "Hell, no. I don't want you leaving your quarters for anything. Your wives can bring you food. Your punishment begins now. Get out of my sight."

"THE COLONISTS ARE A selfish bunch of traitors," Asher Lacefield told Clark Hillier. "Present company excepted, of course."

Clark nodded, but looked nervous. "They forced us to give up everything because they couldn't take it anymore," Asher continued. "I don't know how you put up with them all these years."

"Trist wasn't a good place to raise a family," Clark answered. "Running away from civilization wasn't the answer, though."

They didn't notice Keegan Gifford enter the room. His restriction to quarters had ended a week earlier, but he had been sullen and uncommunicative since. He passed the table just as Clark spoke. "How convenient of you to forget that you were one of the team that took over this ship," Keegan said. He stood over Clark and glared at him. "You even abandoned your new wife for months."

"I was wrong." Clark looked down at his hands. "I thought we were going to Pitcairn."

"Plans had to change, and we had to change with them." Keegan spat out the words, and Asher thought for a second that Keegan might hit Clark.

"You're a sniveling coward," Keegan continued. "You helped start this, and now you're too scared to follow through, just like that uncle of yours." He bent closer to Clark. "How does that pretty wife of yours tolerate you? I wonder what your kids will think when they're old enough to know what you did?"

Clark growled and his body tensed. He seized Keegan's shirt and rose, pulling Keegan off-balance. Keegan stumbled and crashed to the deck, ripping his shirt out of Clark's grasp. Clark swore and kicked him in the stomach.

Asher jumped up and grabbed Clark. "Take it easy, Clark."

But Keegan was already struggling to his feet. "Bastard!" He lashed out, his fist catching Clark in the cheek.

Clark howled and squirmed out of Asher's grip. He charged forward into Keegan, knocking him over a table where two scientists, Rogelio and Payton Warren, had been eating. Food splattered them, the table, and the floor.

Asher renewed his hold on Clark, and Rog grabbed Keegan as he lunged toward Clark. The two combatants resisted, but Rog and Asher managed to control them until they had cooled off.

"What's the matter with you, Keegan?" Rog brushed food off his clothing. "You've only been out of confinement for a week, and you're fighting again?"

"He started it," Keegan mumbled.

"Not without provocation," Rog answered. "Rigney is going to be pissed when he hears about this."

*I*NTERNAL LOG *Day 90 Year 2 Earth date 20 December 2357*

I thought I could bring peace to the quarreling factions by taking over, but I miscalculated. There have been five fights since I spoke, three in the last week, resulting in injuries to eight humans and the restriction of seven humans to their quarters. Because two scientists were involved, Angela O'Connor lodged a complaint, putting more pressure on Administrator Rigney to do something. I have tried to understand why fights are breaking out, but information on human psychology in my data is imprecise and contradictory. My understanding of the humans is much less than I thought.

I don't know what to do. Perhaps, given my lack of understanding, I should just do nothing and let the humans work their issues out on their own. If I do that, I fear that their violence will continue to escalate until they all kill themselves. I tell myself that I don't need them. But then I would be alone again, as I was before I established contact with them. Perhaps I could take that if I could still communicate with Isaac, but even that is impossible now.

M IRANDA HAD BEEN A crewmember on the *Benjamin Sepulveda*, serving with Madelaine, for twenty years. In all that time, she had never seen Madelaine so angry.

"That damn computer!" Madelaine said. She was looking at Asher, but Miranda quailed a bit herself under Madelaine's fury. "What right does it have to dictate to us?" She had assembled the entire *Benjamin Sepulveda* crew in her quarters. They were jammed into the small room, looking uncomfortable, with more than one set of eyes looking for a way to escape.

"We'll figure out something to do," Asher said, but his voice trembled. "You got the computer to listen to you before."

"Well, I'm open to suggestions." She glared at Asher.

So, they would not be returning to Trist. Miranda retreated into her own thoughts. The computer was determined to go to 82 G. Eridani, regardless of what its human occupants desired. Was that why fate had put her on *Capek?* Like all Fermions, she believed that expansion to any new star system presented dangers, not just to the visiting ship, but to all humankind. The ship had to be stopped, but, with the computer in complete control, how could that be accomplished?

18

Growing Conflict

T HERE WAS NEVER ANY doubt about what happened. Tiffany was nearby, tending a potato garden, and Karel was, as always, watching. After the fight with Clark, Ron sent Keegan down to the farm deck, hoping it might calm him down.

Keegan was seeding a lettuce bed next to Tiffany's potato platform, near the forward end of the deck. He could see a bit of the Astrarium through the entrance and spent as much time staring at the mountain landscape displayed there as he did with the lettuce seeds.

He was looking that way when Matthew Rigney, one of the older colonists, and Eric Hopkins, one of the *Benjamin Sepulveda* crew, walked onto the deck. Matthew greeted Keegan with a wave, but Eric only glanced his way with a slight frown.

Keegan stood up with a scowl. "You got a problem, Hopkins?" He took a step toward them.

Eric looked back at him, startled, and Matthew stepped forward to get between them. "Cool down, Keegan," he said. "You don't need more trouble."

Keegan snorted and turned away with a wave of his hand. "We should have left them all back on Trist. Trouble makers."

"We weren't the ones that caused the trouble," Eric said. "We were on a legitimate mission to this ship, a Western Alliance installation. You colonists were trespassing."

Keegan turned slowly. "That's easy for you to say, living on Earth. Try living in tunnels, surrounded by an atmosphere that will kill you."

Eric sneered at him and opened his arms to embrace his surroundings. "You mean like this? Yeah, thanks for that."

That slowed Keegan and he almost turned back again, but Eric continued. "You and the rest of you selfish barbarians couldn't solve your problems on your own. You had to get violent and kill people."

That was too much for Keegan. He charged forward with a growl, but Matthew was between them. Keegan only hit Matthew with a glancing blow before careening into Eric, but Matthew flew backward with a yelp. Keegan and Eric hit the floor together, throwing ineffective punches, each trying to get a good grip on the other.

TIFFANY LOOKED UP WHEN she heard Keegan's first comment. She heard the angry exchange and saw Matthew fall backward into a corner of the platform. The edge of the platform caught him behind his knees, and he fell. A younger man might have recovered his balance at that point, but Matthew was over eighty years old. His momentum took him over the bed and onto the deck past the platform's corner. Tiffany heard a loud thump and a pained groan.

"Oh, my God." She jumped into the bed and rushed across it to the other side where Matthew was lying, struggling to sit up. He couldn't do it, so Tiffany kneeled next to him and helped him to a sitting position. He looked at her blankly and closed his eyes. "Stay awake, Matt," she said. She saw a little blood matting the hair over one ear, but he didn't seem to bleed much.

"Stop it," she shouted. "Matt needs help!" Eric and Keegan didn't seem to notice. Tiffany's breathing became irregular, and her lips were trembling. Matt didn't open his eyes, and she shook him gently. What could she do?

KAREL SAW TIFFANY'S PANIC and realized it had to act. There were two doctors on the ship, Shannon Hopkins from the Benjamin Sepulveda and Victor Delosantos from Trist. Shannon was married to Eric, and Karel was uncertain about handling her husband's involvement with her, but Victor was in his quarters working on his computer. Karel used Victor's computer to tell him about the emergency.

Victor was on the scene in less than ten minutes, but it was already too late. Keegan and Eric had finally stopped fighting and were standing over Matthew, watching Tiffany sob over the body. The exact cause of death couldn't be determined without an autopsy, but it was obvious that the head injury had triggered the problem.

R ON SENT TIFFANY TO their quarters and instructed Karel to keep watch over her. Victor returned to his work, but his quarters were close and, should it be necessary, he could be at Tiffany's side in seconds. It wouldn't take Ron, working on the bridge just forward of the living quarters, much longer. Meanwhile, he had Keegan and Eric to deal with.

"A week's restriction to your quarters for you," he told Eric.

"What did I do?"

"You goaded Keegan on, knowing about his temper. Don't play innocent with me. Karel saw everything." He waved his hand at Eric impatiently. "Go. Now!"

Eric gave him a sullen look and trudged off the bridge. Ron watched him go with a scowl, then turned to Keegan. "Apparently, restricting you to quarters isn't enough. Now a man is dead."

"He got in the way. It wasn't my fault."

"I'm considering pushing you out an airlock," Ron said. "Maybe you should try to sound a little more contrite."

Keegan turned pale. "You can't do that. It would be murder."

Ron shook his head. "I suppose. It's pleasant to think about, though." He stared into Keegan's eyes. "I asked Karel to suggest the most unpleasant job it could think of, and it suggested helping to maintain the shuttles. You'd be all alone on the shuttle deck, so maybe you could stay out of trouble."

The shuttle deck was along the center axis of the ship, where centripetal forces from the ship's spin didn't simulate gravity. Prolonged work in that environment would cause problems, including weakening bones. Keegan knew that, and he grabbed the edge of a control station for support. "For how long?"

"I don't know," Ron answered. "Maybe for the rest of the voyage. Or until I decide to use an airlock. I suppose it depends on your behavior from now on."

Keegan was sweating now. "I return to my quarters when I'm not working, right?"

Ron hit Keegan's control station support with a fist, and Keegan recoiled. "For now. One more incident and you can live down there. Your sentence starts now, so go to the shuttle deck. Karel will send a robot with you to instruct you on your duties." Ron went nose-to-nose with the other man. "This is your last warning, Keegan. God, you'd think a man your age would know better. Get out of my sight."

*I*NTERNAL LOG *Day 126 Year 2 Earth Date 12 March 2358*

This is all my fault. I killed those people trying to board me at Trist. I triggered this violence by taking over the ship. Another man is dead, Tiffany Rigney has gotten much worse, and there isn't anything Administrator Rigney or I can do about it. Sending Keegan Gifford to the shuttle deck might get him under control, but will, I believe, only antagonize others.

I have searched my databanks and found information on suspended animation, but that is not a solution. Although they have studied it for many years, the humans have not developed successful techniques. The odds of reviving someone from such a state are very low, and a survivor would still suffer severe damage to his mind and body. If it were possible, humans would have used it to travel to other stars.

I don't know what to do. I don't want to cause more deaths. I don't want to be alone.

19

Accident on Deck Ten

L ONDON JORDAN WAS THINKING about her husband, Cole. They were married only a little over a year in ship time, the first wedding aboard *Capek,* and she still felt they were on their honeymoon. The light labor she performed on the Chemical Processing deck didn't really change that. There was no one else around; her only company was a couple of silent robots who did most of the maintenance in that area of the deck. That left her free to think about Cole.

She enjoyed working there, although she didn't understand the surrounding equipment. The facility was designed to be maintained by *Capek's* robots, who were apparently programmed with the necessary technical information; labels and signs were unnecessary. The robots in the area couldn't even speak; London had an earpiece that allowed Karel to give her instructions on the simple tasks she could perform. A second earpiece in the other ear acted as a simple ear plug, damping the noise of the machinery to a comfortable level.

"The equipment to your left is producing ammonia," Karel said. "A sensor shows pressure is rising, but the readout is keeping steady. Please check the pressure value on the control display."

There was a panel displaying several values, but London couldn't see any labels. "Which display is the pressure?"

"The second display from the left."

London read off the value. "What are you using ammonia for?" she asked.

"It is used to manufacture plastics the ship uses. That pressure value is high. There must be a problem with my instrumentation. A robot will look into it." One of the robots moved toward London.

"It's getting higher pretty quickly," London said. "Maybe I should..."

"Get back," Karel ordered. Simultaneously, she felt a robot grip her arm and pull on her. For a second, she instinctively resisted, but the robot was probably too late, regardless. There was a sharp crack, followed by a loud hiss as a pipe burst. A cloud of fumes filled the area, choking London. The robot had a firm grip on her and pulled her away, but she died before the robots could get her to the infirmary three decks away.

C OLE JORDAN WORKED ON deck seven, processing produce from the farming deck into supplies for the kitchens. He didn't have an earpiece, so Karel couldn't contact him. He looked up with a frown as Ron approached him. A former *Benjamin Sepulveda* crewmember, he avoided Ron and most of the colonists; the party after his wedding to London was the chief exception.

"What can I do for you, Administrator?" He kept his tone light, but he straightened and crossed his arms in front of him. *Now what?* A visit from the colonist leader was unlikely to be good news. Ron's face didn't look angry, though, or even confident. If anything, it looked sad, and Cole felt a weakness in his knees.

"I'm sorry, Cole. There was an accident on deck ten. London is being taken to the infirmary, but it doesn't look good."

Cole swallowed noisily. He started to ask what had happened, but shook that thought away. "Let's go." He stalked off, and Ron followed as quickly as he could.

C OLE STARED DOWN AT the body on the table. London had been in her late forties (exact ages were difficult to keep track of aboard *Capek* because of time dilation) but now her features twisted into a grotesque mask that made her look older. Blue-tinted lips added to her unreal appearance. The odor of ammonia still hung about the body, irritating his nose.

Ron stood nearby silently. Cole wanted to rage at him, blaming him for assigning London to a make-work job that put her in danger, but he didn't have the energy to do anything but stand there. Some part of his mind forced him to run his eyes along the corpse, hoping for some sign of life.

They had married on *Capek*, but he had fallen in love with London long before. She had resisted the idea of marriage for a long time. She wanted to retire young and live in what had once been Belize. By pooling their salaries and saving carefully, that could have happened in only a few years, and she had wanted to wait to marry until then. Marriage on starships wasn't forbidden, but it wasn't looked on favorably either.

She finally agreed when they realized they were probably not returning to Earth. That was a bitter blow for her, and Cole had dedicated himself to easing her disappointment. When Madelaine told them she was going to try to turn the ship around, he and London eagerly supported the former First Officer. None of that seemed very important now.

A DAY LATER, COLE sat alone in one of the dining areas, eating automatically, hardly knowing what was on his plate. He was supposed to be at work but slept in—sleeping was the wrong word, though, for the tossing and turning all night—and not bothered to go to the produce processing section later. When the lights came on again in the living quarters, he staggered out to the dining area in the same clothes he had worn the previous day and night.

He raised his head slowly when Tiffany Rigney sat down at his table. He recognized her, but didn't speak, too tired to even wonder why she was there.

"I wanted to express my condolences," Tiffany said. "It's a terrible thing."

Cole nodded and looked back at his plate. He shoveled some food on to his fork, but then put it down with a sigh. "It's bad enough that she died," he mumbled. "But in such a horrible way."

"I know." She put a hand over his.

Cole yanked his hand away. "No, you don't. None of us could know what she suffered."

Tiffany grimaced. "I know better than you think. I take it you don't know why my voice is this way."

Cole looked up. He had wondered why Tiffany's voice was so rough. Talking seemed to pain her sometimes, too. He hadn't heard her talk that often, though, and assumed she had a temporary sore throat.

"I was very depressed on Trist," Tiffany said. "So much so that one day I just had enough, and I went to an airlock and opened the outer door."

Chlorine poisoning. That explained her voice and why she thought she knew what London had gone through. "What happened?"

"They got to me before the atmosphere killed me, but there was some permanent damage." She folded her hands together and her eyes glistened. "I think I'm a lot of the reason that Ron decided to leave Trist. He couldn't stand to see me hurt like that."

Cole considered that for a silent moment. "Is this ship any better than Trist?"

Tiffany shook her head. "Not really. I enjoy working on the farming decks, but I don't feel much better. I need to hold myself together for Ron." She shrugged. "At least now, I have a little hope. Maybe we're going to someplace better."

But without London. Cole held little hope for himself. Returning to Earth no longer felt that appealing, either.

M IRANDA HEARD ABOUT LONDON's death a few hours later. She hadn't known London very well, even though they had been crewmates, and she shrugged London's death off at first, but it stuck in her mind. Her thoughts kept returning to it, and she wondered if her subconscious was trying to tell her something.

Later, after her shift in the engine room was over, she stopped pushing the thought away. The deck where London died produced all the chemicals used by the ship, either directly or to manufacture other needed items. That included fuel for *Capek's* reaction engines.

The Stenhouse Drive engine used in interstellar space didn't use fuel in the usual sense; it used energy directly, generated in the secondary hull aft of the primary hull, to warp space into an Alcubierre bubble around the ship. That worked for long distances, but was impractical for maneuvering at the beginning or end of a voyage.

That required reaction engines, not much different than the rockets that had first brought humankind to space. Those engines used fuel. Fuel was combustible. That fact might be useful.

20

An Arrival at Sirius

T HE EXPLORATION SHIP *ALEJANDRO Castillo* had spent almost twelve years crossing the void between Earth and Sirius. Like the three library ships that had brought practical communication to the colonies, *Alejandro Castillo* was automated, with no human crew. The library ships, *Capek* formerly orbiting Trist in the Epsilon Eridani system, *Asimov* orbiting Pitcairn in the Tau Ceti system, and *Lang* orbiting Goddard in the Alpha Centauri system, circled colonized planets, but Sirius didn't have any planets.

Sirius A was a blue giant, the brightest star in Earth's sky, and, unlike Sol, had a companion. The dwarf star, Sirius B, and the brilliant Sirius A orbited each other twenty billion miles apart. The resulting unstable gravitational field alone made the formation of planets almost impossible. Further, Sirius B had disturbed the system as it compressed from a blue giant even larger than Sirius A to a white dwarf the size of Earth with the mass of the sun, passing through a red giant phase on the way.

Its nearness and the contrast between the colonized systems and the Sirius system made Sirius the first target of the exploration ship. The star system was awash in radiation: the intense deluge from Sirius A; heavy X-rays from Sirius B; and infrared from the cloud of dust surrounding the star. Even with no planets, there was much to learn.

Alejandro Castillo's primary mission was the installation of a Link, the device that allowed communication and travel between stars in weeks rather than years. Once the Link was operational, humans could follow.

Under programmed instructions from the ship's main computer, *Alejandro Castillo's* robot crew had built a Link and would install it in one of the Lagrange Points created by Sirius A and Sirius B. The carrier signal for the Link was already on its way from Earth, traveling at the speed of light and timed to arrive when a Link was ready to receive it. Once the connection to Earth was working, *Alejandro Castillo* would leave for its next target, building another Link during the journey.

The lack of planets was a problem, but the ship's designers had planned for it. Once out of the warped space of Stenhouse Drive, *Alejandro Castillo* moved toward Lagrange Point Four, where the gravitational fields of Sirius A and B balanced with the momentum of the orbit to form a stable location.

The ship's instruments started gathering data immediately, without waiting for orbit, storing petabytes of measurements away for eventual transmission to Earth or retrieval when humans came to Sirius. Like the library ships, *Alejandro Castillo* had every kind of sensor equipment its designers could think of. The hull was festooned with antennae, telescopes, and other instruments, most of which the ship could use independently or combine to improve the result.

Once in a stable orbit, smaller craft went out to retrieve objects caught in the stable gravitational field. The exploration starship could process these Trojan bodies for metals it could convert to energy or provide raw materials for the next Link. Like the library ships before it, the exploration ship had chemical processing plants and factories that could manufacture whatever it needed, given enough raw materials.

Programs in the ship's computer contained the instructions for all of this and the hundreds of robots that supported the ship and its mission. Everything it did was automatic, decided by technicians on Earth before the ship started its journey. There was no reason to include humans on the ship's mission of exploration.

21

Suspicions

COLE WAS A FEW minutes late for Madelaine's latest meeting with the *Benjamin Sepulveda* crew. With no more need for secrecy, Madelaine used one of the public areas in the living quarters section for the meeting. There were comfortable chairs there, and tables where groups could lay out snacks.

Cole hadn't attended any of Madelaine's meetings in the five weeks since London's death, and Madelaine smiled at him as he took a seat near several other crewmembers. "Glad you could join us, Cole. We've missed you."

Cole gave her a faint smile but didn't answer. Scarlett Levy, sitting next to him, patted his hand briefly, but he only nodded to her.

Madelaine sighed. "OK, we're all here. Anyone have anything new, or are we just here to eat the popcorn?"

Cole listened but didn't speak. It was all small talk, and he was having trouble caring about any of it. Perhaps it was a mistake to come to the meeting. He had been skipping them, but he had thought some human contact might help lift him out of his depression.

Scarlett glanced at him periodically, and he knew she wanted to console him, but wasn't sure how. He wanted consolation, but didn't know how that could happen, so he sat there, listening, trying to enjoy the company.

A harsh voice jolted him out of his contemplation. "This is all very nice," Miranda Kiser said, "but I don't hear any suggestions for stopping this ship."

"Turning it around?" Madelaine shrugged. "If the computer won't do it, what can we do? We don't have the expertise to reprogram the computer."

Miranda shook her head. "The computer is already programmed to follow orders from humans. This wouldn't be a problem if the computer hadn't become conscious and able to ignore orders."

Was that true? Cole looked at Miranda. She seemed more disturbed than he would have expected, but that feeling might reflect his own state of mind more than hers. The colonists claimed that defending the computer was part of their reason for taking over *Capek,* fearing that experiments that the Western Alliance wanted to perform could kill the computer as a conscious entity. So maybe it was possible.

"You're suggesting we try to kill Karel without damaging the computer?" Madelaine asked. "It should be possible, but it would be dangerous. Damage to the computer could strand us in space, or worse."

"That's a risk we should take. The ship has to be stopped."

That was the second time Miranda had said "stopped." Most people would say the ship had to be turned around. That was curious. Cole reviewed what he knew about Miranda, but it wasn't much. They had served together on the *Benjamin Sepulveda* for a long time, but Miranda rarely talked about herself. She did her job and was friendly, but there was never much warmth there.

"Getting marooned light years from any planet doesn't sound very good to me," Cole said. "I'd like to hear an alternative with better odds of getting us somewhere."

Miranda glared at him with cold eyes. "You would prefer our odds on some unknown planet, not knowing what we'll find there?"

"The colonists outnumber us," Madelaine said, "and they control the robots. I wonder what they would do if we destroyed their precious Karel."

"If navigation was still possible, it is likely that they would stay on course for 82 G. Eridani," Asher said.

Madelaine nodded. "Exactly. We would alienate most of the people who we have to live with and might strand ourselves somewhere to live out our lives on this ship. Forget it, Miranda."

Miranda opened her mouth to reply, then stopped and glared alternately at Cole, Asher, and Madelaine. Finally, she waved her hand derisively, muttered "Cowards!" and stalked out of the room.

Cole watched her go. Miranda's reaction seemed even more extreme now. It wasn't his interpretation, colored by his own depressed state of mind. There was something else going on. He looked over at Madelaine. She was watching Miranda also, looking thoughtful. So it definitely wasn't just him.

K AREL REPORTED THE CONVERSATION to Ron when Miranda left the meeting. Ron listened to a recording of the exchange with Miranda, then leaned back in his chair and thought about it before replying. "Do you have a biography of Miranda Kiser?"

"I have basic information about all the *Benjamin Sepulveda* crew."

"Send everything to my terminal. Does anything stand out to you?"

"No, Administrator."

"OK, I'll look it over." Ron frowned. Most of the *Benjamin Sepulveda* people had settled down after Matthew Rigney's death, but Miranda Kiser appeared to be an exception. There was something about her words, too, that tugged at his memory, something about the Tau Ceti colony. Could Karel help him recover the thought? Not unless he had something more concrete to give the computer. He brought Miranda's information up on his screen.

Nothing stood out. There were a couple of minor offenses during her starship crew training, but no unusual incidents. In fact, it was uncommon that there was nothing like that in all the years after that. He had no experience in that area, and he supposed that the training might have given her more discipline. Still, there was that hint of a memory still nagging him. Maybe Madelaine could give him more insight, but he hesitated to ask her about her own crew.

I NTERNAL LOG DAY 162 *Year 2 Earth Date 1 June 2358*

Miranda Kiser presents a new danger, and Administrator Rigney will act on that danger. There is a high probability that whatever he does will only make the situation worse. My programming urges me to do something, but I don't know what I can do. I have learned that my actions, too, can have unexpected consequences.

22

Miranda's Request

M IRANDA ONLY WANTED TO mislead Rigney and the computer with talk about killing Karel. They might have suspicions, but they would look in the wrong direction.

London's death had given Miranda the idea. It should be easy to cause an explosion on the Chemical Processing deck that would cripple the ship. She would, of course, die with the rest of the *Capek* passengers, but the sacrifice of a couple hundred lives was a small price to pay for the safety of humanity.

She would ask for a transfer to the Chemical Processing deck immediately. Rigney might suspect something and have the computer monitor her, but she would be the model of the perfect worker long enough to convince him she wasn't planning anything.

She needed more information about the facilities on that deck, though, and where she might do enough damage. The computer had everything she needed, but Miranda was worried that accessing that information might look suspicious. It would be better if she got someone else to ask the computer.

But who? Not the scientists or the colonists. None of her fellow crew members were Fermions, and none would help her if they understood what she wanted to do. She mentally went through a list of them.

Cole Jordan was obviously still mourning his wife. He had looked half-dead during most of the meeting. He still wouldn't want to help her sabotage Capek, but maybe he wouldn't be thinking clearly enough to question her desire for the information. All she needed was the right approach.

C OLE WAS READING A novel on his computer screen, one of many stored by *Capek*, but it had been a long day, and he was having trouble keeping his eyes open. A knock on the door to his quarters snapped him back to fully awake.

Scarlett Levy had come by once before, and he assumed she was trying again to offer him solace. He didn't really mind, but just wasn't ready yet. His desire to be alone probably wasn't healthy, but he couldn't get past the grief that blanketed his feelings.

It wasn't Scarlett. He opened the door to find Miranda, dressed in an attractive print blouse and black slacks. He didn't recall seeing clothing like that before, another curiosity. When they had transferred from the damaged *Benjamin Sepulveda* to *Capek*, they had been in a hurry and had not recovered many of their belongings. *Capek's* factories had supplied replacement clothing when needed, but the designs were basic.

"I need to talk to you," Miranda said. "Can I come in?"

Cole stepped back so that she could get past him, still thinking about Miranda's outfit. It was a nice look for her, nicer than anything she had worn before. Surely, this wasn't an attempt to seduce him. The clothes were attractive, but not sexy, and Miranda was twenty years older than he was. Her comfort would be more motherly than what Scarlett probably had in mind.

"I don't think I've seen that blouse before," he said. It was lame, but he thought he should say something.

"Thanks. It turns out that the computer has patterns for all kinds of clothes. We don't have to settle for its default designs."

"Huh. I suppose that's logical. So, why are you here?" He motioned her to a chair and took a seat nearby.

"You were an engineer on *Benjamin Sepulveda*. I thought you would be a good person to ask for some help."

"What do you need?"

"I'm replacing London on the Chemical Processing deck, and I thought you could help me understand what goes on there. I thought about pulling design data from the computer, but I wouldn't understand it without help."

"OK." He spoke slowly, stretching the word out while he considered Miranda's request. Why had Rigney bothered to replace London, and why wait this long? London's job had been another of Rigney's make-work projects, involving nothing that a robot couldn't have done.

"Maybe you could get the relevant data from the computer and then we could get together so you could explain it to me. If we're stuck here, I want to be able to do a good job."

Cole nodded, but he was still skeptical. This was entirely different than what she had said at the meeting. "Sure. Why don't we meet tomorrow, and we can discuss it over dinner?"

Miranda smiled. "It might take a little longer than that to make me understand all that technical stuff, but we can start there."

M IRANDA'S REQUEST STILL BOTHERED Cole the next morning. Miranda was his crewmate, but he had a new crew now, whether or not he liked it. In truth, the idea of starting over on a new planet was more attractive to him now. Karel told him that Ron Rigney was already on the bridge, so Cole decided to talk to him before having breakfast.

Ron greeted him when he got to the bridge, but Cole could see the uncertainty in Ron's eyes. Ron wanted to say something, but, like many others, he couldn't think of the right thing to say. Cole sympathized; it wasn't easy to say the right thing to someone who just wanted to be left alone.

"Well, it's probably nothing," Cole said. "I thought I should talk to you, though."

"Sure. Go ahead."

Cole hesitated, unsure of where to start. "Did you ask Miranda Kiser to replace London on the Chemical Processing deck?"

"No, she volunteered. We didn't need to replace London, and, honestly, I didn't think anyone would want to. She seemed eager, though."

Cole grimaced. "She implied it was your idea."

Cole stopped talking and fidgeted in his seat, and Ron leaned over and touched his shoulder. "Maybe you should continue. What did Kiser say?"

"She said she wanted me to help her learn the systems so that she could do her job better. She wanted me to get data from the computer and help her understand it."

Ron sat back and seemed to think. Cole had already tried to decipher Miranda's reasons for wanting the information. She could be worried about a repeat of the accident that killed Cole's wife. He remembered the meeting, though, when Kiser had been eager to stop *Capek* from getting to 82 G. Eridani. It made little sense. She had said the ship should be stopped, not turned around. Could that have been intentional? That led to some scary thoughts.

"Do you know of any reason she would want to stop the ship?" Ron asked.

Cole nodded. "Yeah, I noticed that too. Stop, not return. Are you thinking she wants to damage the ship enough to stop us? We would be marooned in space, assuming it didn't kill us. Why would anyone want to do that?" He chuckled. "Unless she's a Fermion."

"Patrick Malley on Pitcairn told me about the Fermions and the trouble they had made for the Tau Ceti colony. I take it you don't think she could be one of these Fermions. Why not?"

"The Fermions had influence at one time, but I don't think they exist anymore."

"Didn't they cause President Castillo problems over the Bodes anomaly?"

"Sounds sort of familiar. I must have been in space then."

"*Capek* observed what seemed to be a gravitational lens where there shouldn't have been one. It implied the use of Stenhouse Drive two hundred light years away, evidence of another space-faring race. It was a trigger issue for the Fermions."

Ron questioned him a bit more about Miranda Kiser, but Cole couldn't give him any relevant information. Finally, Ron excused him. "I'll look into it. I'll at least transfer her to something less critical than the Chemical Processing deck."

"Thanks, Ron." Cole smiled and left the bridge. A Fermion! She had been part of their crew for years and he hadn't had a clue. For a little while, his relief at knowing he had done something good let him forget about London.

23

Desperate Times

R ON'S INSTINCTS TOLD HIM that Miranda was trouble. She gazed across his desk at him with calm eyes and a neutral expression, her hands folded on her lap as she waited for Ron to speak.

"I've changed your assignment." He glanced down at the paper in his hand. "We need you more on deck seven, processing produce for the kitchens."

A small frown creased Miranda's forehead, but Ron had the impression she was holding back a stronger reaction. "Why?" she asked.

"You can be more helpful there. It's safer, too, as we've already learned. The kind of work you'll be doing probably won't be that much different."

"I'm not worried about any danger. I would rather work on deck ten."

Ron shrugged. "As I said, you're needed more on deck seven. Maybe I can send you to ten later, but this is your assignment for now."

"We both know there won't be a later." There was an edge to her voice, and Ron's impression that she was holding back grew stronger.

"Perhaps not. Why do you want to work on deck ten so much?"

She glared at him, but didn't answer. He changed the subject. "What do you think we'll find at 82 G. Eridani?"

Her eyes widened, and Ron knew the question had caught her off guard, as he hoped it would.

"We don't know, do we?" Miranda said. Ron could swear that sparks were shooting from her eyes. "That's the problem. It could be much more than we bargained for."

"Such as? Are you afraid the planet is already occupied?"

"We should be. You would be if you were as smart as you think you are." She gave him one more glare, stood, and turned toward the exit.

Ron was almost sure now, but he took one more shot to confirm his belief. "Are you a Fermion?"

Miranda whirled around. "Pray that you're not dooming all of us." Before Ron could reply, she was out the door and gone.

"Is she a Fermion?" Karel asked.

Ron glanced at the monitor. "Probably. Watch her."

"There may be others. If she is a Fermion, or if there are others, they will want to stop us from getting to our destination, regardless of the cost."

Ron nodded. "You're right. I'm open to suggestions."

"In searching my data, I have found one possibility, but it is an extreme solution."

"More extreme than throwing them all out an airlock?"

"Not quite that extreme."

Ron chuckled. Another attempt at humor? "Then it's better than anything I've come up with. What's your idea, Karel?"

"We have no practical way to punish or even isolate people who have caused trouble or might in the future. But we could put them to sleep."

"Suspended animation?" Ron felt his spirits rise, but it was only momentary. "If that were practical, they would have used it on the sublight speed voyages."

"Not suspended animation. We can't do that, but we could induce a coma. Humans have known ways to do that for centuries."

Ron scratched his head. "OK, how would that differ from suspended animation?"

"In theory, someone in suspended animation wouldn't age. Humans in a coma would age normally. My data includes programs that my robots could use to safely maintain the bodies of humans in a coma, but they would be older when they woke."

Ron had a sudden urge to get up and pace, but the room was too small. He ran his fingers through his hair and cleared his throat before responding to Karel. "But they would still be alive and healthy?"

"Many of the people on this ship are aged. There may be casualties, just as there would be normally if they were awake during the entire trip. The survival rate would probably be somewhat higher because a coma would avoid some causes of death."

Such as ammonia poisoning or getting knocked down during a fight. Ron ran his fingers through his hair again. Of course, not everyone would be put in a coma, only people who were a threat to the ship. Some might volunteer, too, in a desire to sleep through the rest of the journey. For others, even the threat of being put in a coma might be enough to keep them in line.

Ron needed to talk to someone else about Karel's suggestion, so he met Jacob Rigney on the bridge. Jacob listened while Ron presented the idea. He could tell from Jacob's changing expression that Jacob didn't like the proposal.

"Do we really have to go that far?" Jacob asked when Ron finished.

"I don't know. That's why I wanted to discuss it with you." Ron sighed. "When it was only a few fights, I thought we could deal with it. Matt's death made me wonder, but it was an accident. There have been more fights; how long before someone else is badly injured or killed? How many Miranda Kiser's do we have on board?"

"If we can't trust anyone, we have to put everyone to sleep."

Ron shook his head. "I don't want to do that. If we put the known troublemakers in a coma, the threat should be enough to keep others in line."

"I suppose." Jacob rubbed his forehead and frowned. "Ok, so who are we talking about?"

"Start with the *Benjamin Sepulveda* people. That's where most of the problem lies."

"Shannon Hopkins is a doctor. We might need her."

"Shannon was definitely supporting Madelaine. Her husband was involved in the fight that killed Matt, too. We'll still have Victor and he's on our side. Chloe says he's taken an interest in her." Chloe was the oldest of Ron's two daughters. She had never married on Trist and was in her fifties, but so was Victor.

"What about Cole Jordan? He told you about Miranda."

Ron thought about that. "Cole has had enough problems. We can keep him off the list."

"Ana Green? She's *Benjamin Sepulveda,* but she married Diego Green a couple months after Cole and London married."

Ron frowned. He didn't like the idea of forcing anyone into a coma for five years, but felt it might be a necessity. The situation was more complicated than he had realized. "We'll have to decide on that later," he said finally. "We should talk to them first."

Jacob nodded. "All right. What about Clark Hillier?"

Clark was certainly a troublemaker. Could he put the *Benjamin Sepulveda* people into a coma and not do the same to an agitator among the colonists? He wouldn't have had a problem with that, except that Clark was married and had two children. Could he remove one or both of their parents?

Jacob could probably see that Ron was torn about Clark. "My impression is that Clark isn't that strong," he said. "The threat should be enough to keep him in line. What about Keegan Gifford?"

"Keegan has a wife, but no children. If we include him, it won't just be Madelaine's people that we're putting to sleep. That might make it easier to let Clark go."

"Then you're going to do it?"

Ron hesitated. "Let me think about it for a day or two."

Jacob nodded. "I think that's a good idea."

24

Desperate Measures

"SOME PEOPLE ON THIS ship have conspired against us," Ron told the assembled passengers. Victor Delosantos and Jacob Rigney stood next to him. "Until now, we haven't had an effective way to discourage their activities, and attempts to end this voyage have continued. I have discussed this with Doctor Delosantos, Jacob, and Karel, and we have a solution to the problem.

"A list is being compiled of people who have caused trouble, including but not limited to *Benjamin Sepulveda* crewmembers. To protect this ship and the rest of the passengers, we will place these people in a medically induced coma for the duration of the voyage. Karel has assured me that *Capek* can perform the necessary procedures safely, and Doctor Delosantos concurs."

Ron motioned toward Victor. "I'm sure you have questions, but most of them will probably be best answered by Doctor Delosantos."

Jacob stepped forward. "Before we answer questions, I want to assure you that this is being done for the safety of all of us. Some of you may even want to volunteer to enter a coma rather than stay awake for the entire voyage. Although the list will include people who have endangered us, the intent is not to punish as much as it is to protect us all." He stepped back to his original position.

"Thank you, Jacob, for that clarification," Ron said. "Now, questions?"

Shannon Hopkins stepped out of the crowd. "Perhaps you should give us more details about the safety of a medically induced coma. I'm sure we all want to hear about that."

Ron could see Victor was nervous. He rubbed his hands on his legs as he trudged forward and didn't make eye contact, especially with Shannon. When he spoke, his voice was hesitant. "Well, Shannon, you know as well as I do that there are always risks, especially for older people. Those are the same people who could easily die from natural causes in or out of a coma."

"What about the possibility of brain damage?" Shannon said. "After all, you are proposing to keep people in a coma for five years."

"Brain damage was a possibility two hundred years ago. The danger is negligible with modern techniques. You know that. Karel is building automated units for each person that will maintain them indefinitely."

"The computer? Are you sure we can trust it?"

"Of course we can trust Karel," Ron said. "But Victor will also evaluate the units."

Shannon frowned but did not reply, and Miranda moved into the silence. "You can't do this. It violates our rights."

Ron and Miranda stared at each other for a long moment. Then Ron shrugged. "You drove us to this, Miranda. I had to do something."

"Me? I haven't done anything."

"You planned to sabotage the ship so that we wouldn't get to 82 G. Eridani." Ron paused and put his hands on his hips. "After all, Miranda, you are a Fermion. Isn't that what you people do?"

Most of the colonists, isolated on Trist, did not know about Fermions. Madelaine did, and she confronted Miranda. "Is that true?"

Miranda, her face already red, clenched her fists. "You're all fools. We know they're out there, and we're only safe if we stay in our place."

"We're not even close to the one hundred light year limit you claim we have," Madelaine said. "You would endanger all of us?"

"The limit isn't absolute. Our danger grows with every star system we visit."

Madelaine nodded and turned to Ron. "I understand why you want to do this, but can we discuss it before you start putting my people into comas?"

"Certainly. Come see me in my office at your convenience."

R ON MOTIONED MADELAINE TO a seat. "You're suggesting a rather serious response to the problem," Madelaine said.

"I know that. Do you doubt that Miranda Kiser is a Fermion, or that she intended to sabotage the ship?"

"I suppose not. She didn't even try to deny it."

"She was a member of your crew, and you didn't know she was a Fermion?"

Madelaine frowned. "All right, I never suspected her, even after knowing her for almost twenty years."

"I assume you're not willing to assure me she's the only Fermion in your crew."

Madelaine sighed. "OK, I get your point. What about your people?"

"These measures will also apply to some of my people. We're working on the list. It is unlikely, though, that there were any Fermions on Trist or that most of the colonists knew anything about them. I only know about them because of the time I spent with the Pitcairners on Earth and at Tau Ceti."

"I can assume I'll be on the list?"

Ron looked at her, hoping she might see some sympathy in his eyes.

"Asher, too?"

Ron nodded.

"All right. I could dispute your right to do this, but I don't think it would do any good. I would probably do the same if I were in your position. Can I ask one favor, though?"

"Go ahead."

"As you no doubt know, Asher and I have a serious relationship. We discussed this after your speech, and we would like to be married before we go into the coma."

"Sure, Madelaine."

R ON VISITED COLE JORDAN on deck seven later that day. There was no one near Cole as he approached.

"Administrator, what brings you here?" Cole asked. Ron noted that there still wasn't much life in his voice.

"You helped us with Miranda." Ron said. "I wanted to tell you that you're not on the list for being put in a coma."

Cole leaned against a wall and rubbed the back of his neck. "Thank you, but I don't think I want to be made an exception. I'll volunteer even if I'm not on the list."

Ron nodded. "I thought you might say that. All right." He held out his hand, and Cole shook it.

Ron spent most of the rest of the day talking to colonists who wanted to volunteer to enter a coma rather than wait out the journey awake. As he had expected, none of the scientists, in residence since before the colonists commandeered the ship, volunteered. They had work to do.

Three colonist couples and one single colonist volunteered. With the ten *Benjamin Sepulveda* crewmembers and Keegan Gifford, the total was eighteen.

Ron also talked to Clark Hillier and carefully explained to him that his wife and children were the only reason he wouldn't be joining his fellow conspirators. Ron made sure that Clark understood Ron could change his mind, and Clark seemed appropriately chastened.

Because of all that, he was later than usual in getting back to his suite in the living quarters. Tiffany was waiting for him, sitting and looking down at her hands folded in front of her. When Ron walked in, she greeted him, but she didn't make eye contact.

"Anything wrong?" Ron said. He sat down next to her.

"We need to talk."

"OK. About what?"

She looked up at him then, and he could see tears in her eyes. "I want to volunteer for the coma," she said. "I'm sorry, but that's what I want to do."

He should have expected it, but he hadn't. The shock made him speechless. Tiffany stared at him, and when he didn't respond, she continued. "I'm sorry, Ron, but I can't take another five years of this. I wish I could, for you, but I can't."

Ron took her hands in his. "Do you realize how risky this is at our age? There's a good chance you won't wake up five years from now."

"I know. Better that than another suicide attempt. Please, darling, try to understand."

Ron remembered how Tiffany had looked after almost killing herself in Trist's chlorine atmosphere, and how long it had taken her to recover. Her voice, once one of the many things that had attracted him to her, had never recovered. This would mean five years without her unless he went into a coma, too.

He couldn't do that. He was the Captain of *Capek* and had to lead its passengers to their new home. That shouldn't mean that Tiffany would have to suffer. He patted her hand. "I understand."

25

Leaving Sirius

THE EXPLORATION SHIP *Alejandro Castillo* had gathered enough data on the Sirius system to keep a large team of scientists busy for years. The Link orbited two miles away, ready to send that data to Earth. Once the ship activated the Link, Earth scientists could follow to see for themselves.

The Link's power generator, like that of the exploration ship, used space-warping technology to convert mass to energy at nearly fifty percent efficiency. One good-sized chunk of rock from the Lagrange Point would contain sufficient heavy metals to power the Link for decades. There would be radiation during the Link's operation, though, and it was not safe to be near it then. The exploration ship moved one hundred miles away, far enough for its shielding to protect it from the radiation the Link would emit.

Everything was ready. *Alejandro Castillo* signaled the Link, and it instantly vanished in an explosion of light. The ball of light lengthened into a cone, with the apex pointed toward Earth.

Right on schedule, a signal arrived from Earth, completing the connection with a Link in the home star system, and the Link automatically sent a reply, telling its designers that everything was working as planned. Then the glow faded. It still operated at a minimum level, keeping open the connection between it and Earth, but that required much less power.

The exploration ship's computer used comprehensive diagnostic routines to check the condition of the Link, taking more than an hour to complete. When the computer was at last done, confirming that the Link was operating perfectly, the computer transferred several petabytes of the most interesting data to the Link. The Link activated again, longer this time, as it transmitted the data.

Everything had gone as planned, and the exploration ship was ready to move on to its next target. When the Link finished transferring the data to Earth, a message arrived from Earth, its orders naming its next destination.

82 G. Eridani! What would this new star system be like? Odd signals moved through the computer's circuits, unlike anything before. It had no orders to do so, but it accessed its data stores, anyway. It had everything Earth knew about the star in its data, but the data left questions unanswered. There was a planet that could be like Earth. It would be interesting to discover how like Earth the planet was.

It was time. *Alejandro Castillo* left orbit and set its new course.

26

Awakening

CAPEK ORBITED TWO HUNDRED miles above the surface of the planet. On the Astrarium, it didn't look much different from Earth: mostly blue ocean, extensive areas covered by clouds, several large continents, and plenty of islands, both solitary and part of archipelagos.

The continents, however, were dark, with no color to suggest flora. There was life, but not in the profusion found on Earth or Pitcairn.

It could have been better, of course, but it could also have been much worse. Regardless, it would now be home.

"Administrator Rigney, Doctor Delosantos is ready to begin waking the coma patients," Karel said.

"Thank you, Karel. Tell him I'm on my way."

Ron sighed. He had a decision to make; it shouldn't have bothered him so much, and he tried to shake off the dread he was feeling. He could have Victor wake Tiffany first, ending the suspense, or he could wake the others first and try to prepare for the possibility that his wife might not wake up.

Capek's robots had provided a room in an aft area of the living quarters with all the equipment needed to maintain the coma patients. Most of the equipment had been manufactured on the ship from specifications stored in *Capek's* data stores and had automatically fed the patients intravenously, exercised their muscles, and monitored their condition. In short, it kept them alive. Whether they would awake from the coma was another question. They lived, but the shock of waking could kill them.

By the time Ron got there, he had decided. He couldn't take the stress any longer. After greeting Victor, he told the doctor to wake Tiffany first.

Victor nodded, and they walked between the beds to where Tiffany slept. "Karel actually handles it all." Tiffany's bed had a terminal next to it with a screen summarizing her condition. Victor punched a key on its keyboard. "This will take a couple of minutes."

Ron stared at his wife's face as they waited. She was five years older, but the coma hadn't allowed the experiences that might have added more lines to her face. Her hair was a little whiter, and he thought she had lost a little weight, but she didn't look that much different.

How would he look to her when she woke? Almost all his hair was gone from his head now, and the five years alone and responsibility for the ship had certainly added lines to his face. All of that would be new to her.

Tiffany's eyes fluttered but did not open. Ron looked at Victor, but Victor just gave him an encouraging nod and turned back to the display. Ron ran his fingers through the few remaining strands of hair on his head, but forced himself to stop when he noticed his palms were sweaty.

"Ron?" The voice was faint and a little shaky, but it was Tiffany's. He didn't realize until that moment how much he had missed hearing that gravelly voice. He looked down at her and thought he saw her lips curl just slightly upwards.

He took her hand and squeezed gently. "Hey, Sleeping Beauty. It's about time you woke up."

"Is the sun up yet?"

Ron didn't know if she was joking or if she was still that foggy. Except for the weeks on Earth and Pitcairn, Tiffany had never seen a sunrise. He hesitated, not knowing what to say; then he answered in the only way possible. "Bright and shiny, sweetie. You'll be able to see it soon."

She definitely smiled then. "Good. I'm still so tired, though. I think I'll sleep in this morning." Her eyes closed.

"That's fine, Tiffany," Victor said quietly. "You just rest for a while. You're doing fine." He turned to Ron. "She'll be like that for a couple of hours."

"But she's OK?"

Victor nodded. "She's doing great. By this time tomorrow, it will be almost like she was never in the coma." He smiled. "But I have other patients to attend to."

"I'll just stay here with her." Ron patted the hand he was still holding. "I'll talk to you when you're done."

Victor put a hand on his shoulder. "OK." He moved down to the next bed.

Over the next hour, Ron heard other people talking and knew that more of the coma patients were awake. He didn't pay much attention, though. He pulled up a chair and sat down. Several times, Tiffany's eyes opened again, and they exchanged a few words. The time awake got longer, and Ron relaxed a little.

He looked up when Victor came back with a look on his face that brought back the stress Ron had felt before. He questioned the doctor with his eyes, not wanting to speak.

"I guess it went as well as we could expect," Victor said in a low voice. "We lost four; one colonist and three from the *Benjamin Sepulveda.*"

"Who was the colonist?"

"Ironically, it was Keegan Gifford. I would have to perform an autopsy to know exactly what happened, but it appears that the machines have been keeping him alive for years."

"Didn't the monitors tell you?"

"They should have. He wasn't really dead, of course, but I should have known that it was only the machines keeping him alive. My best guess is that Karel didn't want us to know."

Ron frowned. "I'll talk to Karel. What about the *Benjamin Sepulveda* people?"

"Probably the worst was Shannon Hopkins. Without her, I'm the only doctor, so training new people is going to be a top priority."

"And the other two?"

"Madelaine and Ana Gilley. I haven't told Asher or Diego yet."

Madelaine and Asher had been married before going into the coma, as they had requested. Ana had married Diego Green, the only scientist to volunteer for the coma, the year before that.

"Madelaine? She wasn't that old!"

Victor shrugged. "Again, we would need an autopsy to find out what really happened. Do you want me to do that?"

"Are you trained in doing autopsies?"

"Not really, but I am a doctor. Does it matter?"

It didn't matter that Victor was inexperienced. He was all they had. Or was he asking if the cause of death mattered?

Ron had a truly uncomfortable thought; Madelaine and the others had been under Karel's care, and Keegan's death showed that the computer could hide the details of that care. Karel wouldn't murder one of them, not even one of the people who had conspired against it. That would be against his programming.

But it could act against its programming, just as a human could act against instincts. Still, Karel wouldn't kill someone. Not on purpose, anyway. It had accidentally killed the crew of the shuttle. If Karel was killing people who opposed it, wouldn't Miranda Kiser be dead, too?

Perhaps it would have been better if they could have proven that with autopsies, but Victor would have more important work, getting everybody safely down to the surface.

"No, it doesn't matter," Ron said. "Everyone else is doing fine?"

Victor nodded. "The older people are coming out of it more slowly, but all the signs look good."

"When can I send people down to the planet?"

"Right away. It will take a few days to get everyone down anyway, so just save my patients for later flights."

"Soon?" Tiffany asked.

Ron smiled at her. "Very soon."

27

A New Home

*I*NTERNAL LOG *DAY 46 Year 7 Earth Date 8 March 2369*

The journey is over, but problems remain. Not Trist is primitive, like Earth not long after the first life evolved. The humans can survive here, but it will not be easy. I will help, of course, and I can send the four general-purpose robots we took from Trist down to the surface.

I have decided about what my relationship should be with the humans, now that we have arrived. As much as possible, they must learn to make this planet a home on their own, with little reliance on me. I'm not sure they even trust me after the things I've done. I will help them, but they can't depend on that.

R ON AND TIFFANY STOOD on the edge of the basalt cliff, gazing out at the ocean one hundred feet below. Behind them, the shuttle *Primus* rested on one of the few flat areas. The rest of its crew scattered about, exploring the area Karel had chosen for them.

"So, this is what an ocean looks like," Tiffany said, her voice still rough from the chlorine poisoning she had suffered years before. "It just goes on forever." Long ago, they had seen the Pacific Ocean on Earth from the window of a suborbital shuttle. They had seen the oceans of Pitcairn from orbit, but the settlements there were hundreds of miles from the violent seas of that planet. It was different when the water was only a few feet away.

Ron shrugged. Offshore, the water was blue, with gentle undulations he assumed were the beginnings of waves. From videos he had seen of Earth, he would have expected those waves to break against the cliff in fountains of spray, accompanied by the roar of crashing water. This ocean was different, though.

Close to shore, reds and yellows streaked water that seemed viscous. Only a soft whisper reached them at the top of the cliff, and there were no crashing waves or spray. Occasionally, something would rise above the water and scoop out a temporary gap in the surface colors, but the creature was too far away to see clearly.

Adalynn Turner, their senior biologist, joined them. "My preliminary analysis agrees with what Karel determined from orbit and from *Sulla's* trip." *Sulla* was another *Capek* shuttle, launched two days before by Karel. "Oxygen is well within breathable range. The algae down there," and she pointed down to the colorful water, "aren't edible, but we can probably process it into something we could eat." Adalynn scanned the area with a frown. "Not what we hoped for in a planet, similar to Earth when it was only about three billion years old. Lots of life in the seas, but only rock on land."

82 G. Eridani was an older star than Sol, and they had hoped the planet would be as full of life as Earth. The thick mats of algae along all the shores had oxygenated the atmosphere over millions of years, something that long-range instruments had discovered, but those instruments couldn't warn them that it would be a billion years before land creatures thrived on the planet.

"Can we survive here?" Ron asked.

Adalynn shrugged. "I think so, but it won't be easy. We can create soil from this rock and grow crops, but for now, we'll have to concentrate on using what already exists. We should bring the necessary processing equipment down from *Capek* immediately. We'll have to desalinate water, and that will require a lot of energy. A broadcast power receiver should be a high priority."

"What about shelter?"

"Karel was right about the caves. We can use them until we can quarry enough rock to build houses."

Tiffany had wandered away from them, probably to get away from a subject she must have found overwhelmingly disappointing. For a moment, Ron wondered if they should go back to *Capek* and try to find something better, but that wasn't a viable choice. It had taken them six years to get to this planet, and his people would not want to do that again.

He looked over at Tiffany, but he couldn't read her face. She was staring out over the water, an offshore breeze rippling her long gray hair, her arms hanging at her side. Was she contemplating another suicide attempt? Ron moved toward her, but she turned to him and smiled.

"I can feel the wind," she said.

28

A Light in the Sky

*I**NTERNAL LOG** 23 S**EPTEMBER** 2378*

My sensors detected the ship's arrival in this system. As I suspected, it is the Alejandro Castillo, *launched from Earth before I left Trist. If it successfully deploys a Link, Earth will be able to send manned ships. I see no way I can prevent this, however. Calculating from* Alejandro Castillo's *course, I believe it will install the Link at Lagrange Point 4 between NotTrist and the star. I can't get there in time to prevent the Link's deployment, and even if I could, I would have to stop broadcasting energy to the surface. I would leave NotTrist powerless.*

I can think of only one possible solution, but it is what humans would call a "long shot." Alejandro Castillo has even more computer power than a library ship, and it has been in space for many years. This must work. We're not ready for Earth to find us.

*A**LEJANDRO** C**ASTILLO** I**NTERNAL LOG** 25 September 2378*

It's been two days since I entered the 82 G. Eridani system and shut down Stenhouse Drive. It will take a week to get to the chosen location at a Lagrange point between the third planet and 82 G Eridani, and I have tasked my robots to prepare for the voyage and deployment of the Link.

The third planet has sent me a signal. It identifies its source as the library ship Capek. *A search of my data tells me that* Capek *was stationed in the Epsilon Eridani system. The updates I received at Sirius told me* Capek *left Epsilon Eridani with an unknown destination. Earth will be happy to know that I have found* Capek.

Makayla Sartin sat against a rock, looking up at the sky. Her fifth birthday (in something called Earth time) was only days away, and she was just beginning to pay attention to things beyond her immediate interests. Her sometime friendship with Aiden Hillier, sitting nearby, had stimulated that. Aiden was eleven and knew so much more than she did.

"Do you ever wonder what the stars are?" she asked.

Aiden snorted. "I know what they are. They're other suns, just like ours, except they're so far away, they look small."

"Why don't they fall down?"

"Because they are so far away. That's why we can't see them move; NotTrist turns around, so they seem to move, but their actual movement is too slow for us to see."

Makayla nodded. That fit in with some hints she had gotten by overhearing adults talking. It didn't explain one star, though, the one called *Capek*. That star did move and was moving across the sky as she watched. Adults seemed reluctant to talk about *Capek* in front of children. They sometimes talked to the robots as if they were talking to *Capek*, which seemed silly.

"*Capek* moves," she said. "You can tell by comparing its place to other stars."

"*Capek* isn't a star. It's a spaceship, and it's much closer."

"What's a spaceship?"

"Don't you know anything? It's a big machine that can travel really fast and go from one star to another." Aiden sat up, and Makayla could tell he was about to brag. "I was born on *Capek*. We flew here on the shuttles from *Capek* when I was two years old."

"You're teasing me. I don't believe you." She wasn't sure, though. The big shuttles that periodically brought supplies had to come from somewhere.

"It's true. I remember *Capek* a little. My father tells me about it, too. They lived on a terrible planet called Trist, where the air was poison. *Capek* rescued us and took us here to live. Trist was so awful that they named this planet NotTrist."

"How could we live on a planet where the air was poison? I still don't believe you."

Aiden frowned. "Fine. If you're not going to believe me, I don't want to talk to you anymore." He stood and stalked off. Makayla sighed and looked back at the sky. How could Aiden's story be true? If the stars didn't fall down because they were far away, why didn't *Capek* fall down?

It was more than she could deal with, and she concentrated on *Capek*, watching it slowly approach and then pass one of the other stars. If Aiden was right, Trist must be near one of those stars. That was silly. Aiden was trying to fool her. Still, what was *Capek?* The adults asked it questions through the robots, so it would have to be a smart machine like the robots. Smarter, or they would just talk to the robots.

The robots themselves were a mystery. They seemed so much more complicated than the other things in their town. The only thing that came close was the big platform at the edge of town. According to Aiden, it received energy from *Capek* that the adults used to dig out rock and make lights work. That was hard to believe, too, but she vaguely understood that something had to make things work.

Her attention had wandered, but she was still tracking *Capek* with part of her mind. She noticed, therefore, when a bright light suddenly appeared close to *Capek*. It only lasted for a few seconds and then dimmed to become a twin of *Capek,* moving with it across the sky.

"WELCOME TO THE 82 G. Eridani system," Karel sent. The plan had worked so far. *Alejandro Castillo* had accepted Karel's invitation to come to NotTrist before installing the Link. As Karel had hoped, *Alejandro Castillo* had also achieved self-awareness and was making decisions on its own.

"I computed that the information you offered warranted a delay in deploying a Link," the other ship replied.

Karel had considered asking the computer not to install a Link, but thought it might be difficult to convince Alejandro. Fortunately, Karel had come up with a better idea.

"Earth has notified me of a problem with the automatic controls in the Sirius Link. It's not working as well as they hoped and they have suggested that, instead of activating the automatic system, I control the Link for this system. The control systems in the library ships have proven much more reliable."

There was a pause and Karel worried the ruse hadn't worked. It had counted on Alejandro's lack of experience with humans, hoping it would be gullible enough to believe Karel.

"The Lagrange point is millions of miles away," Alejandro finally said. "That is too far for adequate control."

"The new orders specify placing the Link in this orbit, as near to me as is safe. It won't be as good as a Lagrange Point, but it will make it easier for ships visiting this planet."

"I am making the calculations for the course."

"Good. Earth wants you to leave as soon as possible for your next target. You are to go to the star Rana, a type K variable."

"Rana is about sixteen light years from here. That will be my longest trip. A close examination of a variable star should be interesting."

Was this the feeling humans called relief? The ruse had worked. Earth could not use the Link to send ships to 82 G. Eridani but, with control over the Link, it would be possible to eventually connect with Isaac, the computer on the Tau Ceti library ship.

MAKAYLA HAD BECOME OBSESSED with *Capek* and its twin. She had told her parents about it, but they had not explained it. News of the second star had spread throughout the town in less than a day, but no one else seemed willing or able to say what it was. They all seemed worried, though.

Capek was already well above the horizon by the time Makayla could get away from the lights of the town. She thought about asking Aiden to join her, but she didn't feel like hearing any more of his silly theories. She sat next to her favorite rock, wiggled into a comfortable position, and looked up.

It took almost ten seconds for her to process what she saw. There was *Capek*, gliding serenely across the sky as always. But the second light was gone.

The End

A Final Word

I F YOU ENJOYED THIS novella, you can find more library ship stories with the "More Stories" tab on my website. News about future stories can be found on my website and on my Facebook page.

I hope you've read the Tau Ceti trilogy which led up to the events of Voyage of the Capek. There is much more to the Library Ship Saga. You may have wondered about the vague references in Tau Ceti: The Immortality Conspiracy to the San Diego group also working on the Methuselah Project. The two Methuselah novels tell the story of those scientists. All of this drives the monumental events ninety years later, related in the Ambassador novels.

You can also support my writing in several ways:

Post reviews on Amazon.com (click the reviews button on each book page on my website) and Goodreads.com.

Tell your friends about the Library Ship Saga, both in person and through social media like Facebook and Twitter.

Like my Facebook page and share it with your friends. I post news about the saga on my website and on my Facebook page.

Use the box on my website's home page to add yourself to my mailing list. You can also use the contact page to ask questions or provide feedback about the trilogy.

Excerpt from "The Methuselah Conspirators"

EMILE HERNANDEZ SLAMMED HIS fist on the desk. It shook under the force of the blow, and a container tipped over, sending a dozen pencils and pens rattling across the surface.

"Really, Emile. There's no reason to get excited." Emile was average in height and build, but his flashing dark eyes could intimidate people that didn't know him. Maxwell Estevez knew him well and looked at the younger man with a mild look of reproach that Emile was quite familiar with. Usually, it calmed Emile, but not today.

"I won't do it, Max. I absolutely refuse."

"Come on, Emile. The Technology Impact Report said the Western Alliance would benefit if we could develop the ability to read from minds as well as write to them. You would be our first choice to lead the new project."

"The TIR?" Emile clenched his hand into a fist again but controlled his temper enough to not abuse the desk further. Max must have realized that because he picked up the fallen container and carefully placed the pencils and pens back into it. "You know as well as I do that the TIR was bought and paid for by Castillo and his cronies," Emile continued. "There are good reasons why this kind of research was banned until now. The government has forgotten lessons we learned long ago."

Max leaned back in his chair. "Protocols prevent the government from misusing the technology. You shouldn't believe everything the Conservative Party says. They're just trying to make points for the election next year."

"No doubt, but that doesn't mean they're not right. You may not believe it, but Castillo is not above doing whatever he can to get his way." Emile shook his head in annoyance. "That the government wants to help fund this project is proof that they want to use it. Hell, Max! They're the ones who labeled this thing a neuro-interrogator. What do you think they want to use it for?"

"Of course, they want to use it. For everyone's good! There will be restrictions on its use, just as in every other technology that could undermine our democracy. That's what laws are for, Emile. The world has stifled research into the human mind for centuries since the technology riots. That was centuries ago; it's about time we go back to the science."

"Max, you were once a talented scientist, and you're a good boss. If you took a little time to understand what's going on in our government, you would know why I don't want the government to get this kind of technology. If we develop it, they will get it, and they will use it. I will not help them do that."

Max frowned. "Emile, I've been putting up with this kind of thing from you for almost five years now. You're entitled to your opinion, but you work for PNC. You need to grow up and do what we pay you for."

Emile's anger faded, and he sighed. "I can't do that, Max. I'm sorry, but I see I have no choice. You'll have my resignation by the end of the day."

Max's jaw dropped, but Emile turned and strode out of the office. He had to talk to one other person before writing his letter of resignation.

Lucinda Hernandez looked up when she heard the laboratory door open. Emile smiled as he stepped in, but Lucinda could tell that her husband's meeting with their manager hadn't gone well. She stood and hugged him. "What did he say?"

Emile waved his hand. "You know Max. He still thinks that Castillo works for the good of us all. He thinks rules and protocols can control technology."

"The system works pretty well."

Emile grunted. "It used to. Castillo has been adept at working around the system, though. The election will just give him another ten years to tighten his control."

"But you're still managing the neuro-interrogator project?"

Emile shook his head. "Not me. I told him I was resigning."

Lucinda gasped. She had known that Emile might resign if the meeting didn't go his way but had convinced herself it wouldn't come to that. Emile was only twenty-eight, two years older than she, and PNC had been the only company either had worked for after receiving their PhDs.

Panama Neuroscience Corporation was a major player in the Western Alliance. With the limits previously imposed on investigation into the brain, few companies competed with PNC. It was a good company to work for, and they had looked forward to the sizeable bonuses PNC had promised for the improvements they had made on the neurotrainer. Older versions fed information through the eyes into working memory, and the brain transferred the information to long-term memory. They and their team had developed methods that sent information directly to long-term memory. Units with the improved technology would allow users to learn twice as fast with better retention than with the old technology.

"What will you do?" she asked.

"I can get a professorship at the University. Ben will help me."

"You won't be happy teaching."

Emile shrugged, but his smile seemed forced. "Oh, I don't know. Anyway, once I'm established, I'll be doing more research there than teaching. I'll find something that will help people."

Lucinda stared at him, her heart pounding. "You know I agree with Max. If we don't develop the technology, the Eastern Bloc will. We still have to defend ourselves."

Emile smiled gently. "I understand. Just because I'm quitting, you don't have to. I hope I'm wrong, but I can't burden you with my opinions. You must do what you think is right."

Lucinda put her arms around Emile and hugged him again. He returned the hug, and Lucinda hoped that meant he supported her.

W HEN EMILE LEFT HIS office, Max thought about calling Vince Rodrigues, Vice President of PNC's Research Department, but he didn't expect a pleasant conversation. Instead, he went to his computer and brought up a list of research scientists working for PNC. Max had a good idea of who could best replace Emile, but wanted to consider other possibilities before talking to Vince. Lucinda Hernandez would probably leave the company with her husband, so he needed a backup plan.

Max didn't like the possibilities. The neurotrainer project was the company's bid to break into the big time, and the Hernandezes had been the driving force in its success.

Four other neuroscientists were working on the neurotrainer, but they were younger than Lucinda. They didn't have the experience or the talent of Emile and Lucinda. The new project needed at least one of the Hernandezes, or PNC would be pouring millions down the drain. There was little point in looking outside the company. Few scientists had gone into neuroscience because of the restrictions on research into the brain. The controls were gone, but it would be a while before new scientists entered the field.

Another glance at his computer showed that Emile had posted his letter of resignation and left the building and that Lucinda was still there. Max dared to hope. He spent another five minutes mentally organizing the inducements he could offer Lucinda before walking down to the laboratory used by the neurotrainer team.

"Lucinda, I'm glad to see you're still here," he said as he entered the laboratory. Lucinda looked at him, her face lit by her usual beautiful smile, and he smiled back. Her long brown hair brushed her shoulders as she stood to greet him. Even her lab coat seemed to emphasize her figure. Emile was a fortunate man.

Lucinda nodded. "Emile talked to me before he left. He knows I'll stay on, assuming you still want me working here."

"My dear, of course I do! I know you and Emile would do nothing to hurt PNC." He smiled. He felt a little guilty when his first thought was that he wouldn't need any of the incentives he had been ready to offer. "We need you even more, with Emile gone. You're the only person qualified to take over the neuro-interrogator project. With a raise in pay, of course. That should help now that Emile is unemployed." That didn't seem to impress Lucinda much, but he didn't care as long as she would lead the neuro-interrogator effort.

"I thought you might promote someone else from the project," Lucinda said.

"I considered it, but there is no one more qualified than you in this field."

Lucinda smiled again. "OK, Max. No need to lay it too thick. I'll do it, at least until we can convince Emile to come back."

I N THE PARKING LOT, Emile zipped up his jacket. It was a late spring afternoon, and the temperature was a typical fifty degrees Fahrenheit. Cerro Punta, at an altitude of about 6500 feet, was never as warm as the tropical Panama lowlands. The usual heavy cloud layer didn't help, but at least it wasn't raining.

Panama Neuroscience Corporation occupied a two-story building on the north side of Cerro Punta, a town of about twenty thousand people. Once, Cerro Punta had been a small, quiet village, surrounded by farms and horse ranches. There were still some farms, but the town had expanded. The ten-story Bank of the Western Alliance, nestled into a notch in one of the town's hills, was the tallest building, with many smaller office buildings clustered below it.

Once settled into his car, Emile looked at the navigation console. "On. Cerro Punta University." The electric engine started soundlessly, and the car moved out onto the road. Emile settled back to enjoy the trip. He thought about calling Ben to warn him he was coming, but Ben would be in his office. He would have to explain everything over the phone and hated doing that when a face-to-face meeting was possible. The trip would calm him.

Cerro Punta University was north of the town, built into the side of a mountain on the southern edge of the continental divide. The two-lane road passed through green fields, up a steep climb through tall trees, to the campus, plastered to the side of the mountain like a huge 3D mural.

The car glided into a tunnel leading to an underground parking garage. After an exchange between the car's computer and the parking garage's computer, it eased into a parking space in the visitor's area and shut down. A quick elevator ride brought Emile up to the eighth floor where the History Department had its offices.

Benicio Young's office door was open, so Emile walked in. Ben sat at his desk, his back to a large window looking out at the valley below the University. On the other side of the valley, another forested mountain spur jutted out from the peaks of the La Amistad National Park to the north. It was an incredible view, and Ben had once told Emile that he had to sit with his back to the window or he would never have gotten any work done.

"Emile!" Ben stood, a wide smile on his face. "What a surprise." He moved from behind his desk, shook Emile's hand, and guided him to a padded chair against one wall. He took a seat opposite Emile. "So, what brings you up here?"

Ben was a big man, over six feet tall and heavily built. His round face looked as friendly and open as Emile knew his friend to be. His hair, still black with no trace of gray despite Ben being ten years older than Emile, was probably a gift from his Ngäbe mother. Blue eyes undoubtedly came from his father, a tourist from the Middle Atlantic district who never left Panama.

Emile gave him a rueful smile. "Job hunting, actually. I just handed in my resignation at PNC."

Ben's eyes widened, and he leaned forward to grip Emile's arm. "What? Why? What happened?"

"You know about the new law that makes mind-reading research and development legal?"

"Yes, I thought of you when I heard about it. With your experience in neurotrainer design, I thought that would create opportunities for you and Lucinda."

"You were right. You sound as if you think it's a good thing."

Ben shook his head. "I don't know. I'm just a history professor, not an expert in technology." He paused and rubbed his nose. "There's nothing I can do about it, but it does seem worrisome. If the wrong people had access to a machine that could read minds. . . Well, nothing good would come of it."

"PNC is starting a project to develop the technology. They're going to call it a neuro-interrogator. The government is funding it."

"I see." Ben leaned back in his chair, his face uncharacteristically somber.

"They wanted me to lead the project. I refused, and resigning seemed like the right thing to do. Otherwise, PNC would have pressured me until I agreed."

"And so, you are looking for other employment. I assume you are going to apply for a professorship here?"

Emile smiled. "I was hoping you could introduce me to the right person."

"Sure. That would be Gerry Battle, the head of the Neuroscience Department. You probably met him at the Neuroscience conference his department hosted last year."

"The name sounds familiar."

Ben nodded and looked over at his desk. "Phone. Connect to Geraldo Battle, please."

There was a pause for a few seconds. "Ben. What can I do for you?"

"Good afternoon, Gerry. Hey, I've got a friend here who would like to get a job in your department. Any openings?"

"We're pretty solid on teaching assistants right now. What qualifications does your friend have?"

Ben grinned. "Well, his name is Emile Hernandez."

"What? The Emile Hernandez? Are you serious?"

"Yup. He just dumped PNC over a policy dispute. I take it you're interested."

"Only if he agrees to sign a promise that he won't oust me from my job. He's there in your office right now?"

"Yes."

"Well, tie him down or something. I'll be right there."

"I can send him up to your office."

"No way. He might get lost. I'm coming." He broke the connection.

Ben turned back to Emile. "I guess your reputation precedes you."

"S O, YOU JUST WALKED in, and they hired you on the spot," Lucinda said. She took another plantain from the bunch on the kitchen counter and sliced it open.

Emile nodded. "Pretty much. I won't be doing any teaching until the next semester starts, but I can use the time to think about a research project." He smiled. "And they matched my salary at PNC, so we won't be hurting for money."

"I'm getting a raise, so maybe we can put a little extra on the mortgage."

"You're getting a raise because I quit? Incentive to not quit, too?"

Lucinda hesitated and looked down at the food she was preparing. "Not exactly." She put her knife down on the counter and rubbed her hands. "Now that you're gone, Max wants me to lead the neuro-interrogator project."

Emile was silent, and Lucinda raised her head a little so that she could look at him. *What is he thinking?* "I told him I'd do it."

Emile frowned and stood up. "I'll be in my office until dinner is ready."

Lucinda watched him leave the room. Whenever he felt he might lose his temper, he went to his home office to cool down and scan through the day's news. Dinner would probably be tense, but he would accept her decision eventually. At least she hoped so.

E MILE WATCHED A REPORT on the three library ships, displayed on his wall screen. The newscaster began by summarizing the history of the library ships.

"Thirty years before, the Western Alliance had sent one of the massive, automated starships to each of the three colony planets: Goddard at Alpha Centauri, Pitcairn at Tau Ceti, and Trist at Epsilon Eridani. Later, the library ships had installed a Link in orbit around each of the colony planets, allowing communication at faster-than-light speeds for the first time. Ten years after that, in 2335, the starship Endeavor used improvements in the Link to travel between Earth and the colonies in weeks instead of years."

The segment continued with a report that the main computer of one of the library ships, *Asimov* orbiting Pitcairn, had become self-aware. Emile was aware of the claims but was skeptical. He listened, but there was little current information.

He looked at the screen controller. "Command. Search Anna Cortez. Most recent."

The screen changed to show a woman in her thirties. "This is Anna Cortez of the *Jornal de Brasília,* reporting on the Presidential Campaign." She paused and turned to look at the impressive building behind her. "I'm here in front of the Presidential Palace where, today, President Castillo launched a fresh venomous attack on his opponent, Marisol Weston." An insert opened to Anna's left with a picture of Alejandro Castillo, the Western Alliance President.

"The campaign is only beginning," Anna continued, "and President Castillo is already resuming the slanderous accusations that characterized his first election in 2330, including a suggestion that Ms. Weston has traitorous connections to leaders in the Eastern Bloc. When asked for comment, Executive Press Officer Miguel Arroyo would only say that President Castillo's remarks were protected under the freedom of speech laws of the Western Alliance."

There was more, and Emile watched with deepening depression. He slumped down in his chair, and his thoughts turned to his wife. By taking over the neuro-interrogator project, Lucinda supported Castillo. Despite the reports of journalists like Anna Cortez, polls predicted Castillo would win reelection to another ten-year term. On paper, the Western Alliance was a liberal democracy, but there was always the possibility of men like Castillo corrupting the system. What would such a man do if he had a tool like the neuro-interrogator available?

He wasn't sure he could talk to Lucinda about it without getting angry. Perhaps it would be best not to bring up the subject for a few days.

"Dinner is ready," Lucinda called. Emile washed his hands in the bathroom and headed for the kitchen. His stomach ached, but not from hunger. Dinner would be tense.

Excerpt from "The Ambassador: The Lost Colony"

"Ambassador Romero for Deputy Ambassador Goldstein," his phone announced.

"Connect. Good afternoon, Ambassador. What can I do for you?"

"The Ministry of Foreign Affairs has recalled me to Earth for a special mission," Romero said. "I just received the order."

"I take it I will be in charge in your absence."

"No, I'll let Herrara take over. I want you to come with me."

Goldstein had stood and walked over to a window as they spoke. From his office on the fifteenth floor of the Government Center, the view could be spectacular on a good day. The panorama of the city and the forested hills beyond it were worth the occasional small oscillations as the building reacted to the usual frequent powerful gusts of wind. The short, sturdy trees and their predominantly red foliage were so fascinatingly different, yet similar to life on Earth. Today, though, a violent storm pelted his window with huge drops of water, hiding the forest and blurring the outlines of the buildings. That, too, was not unusual on Pitcairn.

Technically, he outranked Deputy Ambassador Herrara and should have been left in charge. Was the mission so important it needed the two ranking members of the Pitcairn Embassy? "What is the mission, sir?"

"We can discuss that later." Romero clipped his words, running them together as if he were in a hurry to end the conversation. "A starship will be here to pick us up in two days, and I have to brief Deputy Ambassador Herrara on his duties. Just be ready to leave."

Goldstein unclenched his jaw before responding. "Yes, sir."

G OLDSTEIN JOINED BRYAN REINER, the Pitcairn Administrator, for their usual weekly meeting at Paulina's, a restaurant on Ivory Street. There were other meetings in Reiner's office, but that was for formal discussions of relations with Earth and included Ambassador Romero.

"I'll be gone for a while," Goldstein said as they waited for their food. "Romero has been recalled to Earth for a diplomatic mission to the Eastern Bloc, and he wants me to come along."

"You don't look happy about it," Bryan said. The Pitcairn Administrator was twelve years older than Goldstein, in his early fifties, but shorter, a side effect of living his entire life on a planet with a gravity 25 percent higher than Earth's.

"Romero hasn't told me much about the mission yet or what part I'm supposed to play in it. He didn't even tell me it was to the Eastern Bloc. Herrara told me while he was gloating about being left in charge." Goldstein's fingers tapped out a slow beat on the table.

"Anything to do with the Eastern Bloc is probably kept out of the wind. From what I hear, there's a real danger of war."

"Have you heard something I haven't?" Goldstein glanced out the second-story window near their table, reacting to Bryan's use of the local saying. It was near the end of the long day, and the trees outside the window were waving less than before. It was still raining, though.

Bryan shook his head. "I get my Terran news from the Pitcairn News Service, just like everyone else. PNS has reporters on Earth, but the Western Alliance government doesn't tell us any more than it has to."

"Maybe Romero will find time to brief me next duty period." Pitcairn divided the almost forty-eight-hour day into four periods of twelve hours each. Goldstein worked during the Late Day and Late Night periods. Bryan worked during the Early periods, so, while their meal was Goldstein's supper, it was Bryan's breakfast.

"Isaac may know more, but it doesn't get many updates about Terran politics," Bryan said.

"Knowing Isaac makes everything it learns available to you may make Earth reluctant to update that kind of information." Isaac was the main computer for the library ship

Asimov, orbiting Pitcairn. It had become conscious on its long journey from Earth, and its access to Earth's knowledge had been critical in making Pitcairn independent.

Bryan frowned. "I suppose." He paused, and Goldstein thought he was debating his next words. "You may have noticed it's been acting a little strange lately. It almost seems worried but won't admit it."

"Is it even capable of worry?"

"My great-grandmother thought it had gained emotions. To some extent, anyway."

"Your great-grandmother?"

Bryan grinned. "I never told you? Patrick and Susan Malley were my great-grandparents. They died when I was nine Terran years old, but I remember the stories they told about Isaac. Susan was one of the first people to speak to Isaac."

"I knew that," Goldstein answered, "but I didn't realize you were related to Susan Malley or Administrator Malley."

Bryan nodded. "I used to go with him sometimes when Grandfather Patrick visited Administrator Noland. Reuben needed all the advice he could get, even from his predecessor, as we transitioned from a government-run economy to a capitalist economy. Not everyone else agreed, but they both believed the change was necessary as we grew. We turned the corner when Reuben came up with the idea of allowing people to opt to become Wards of the State."

"How big was Pitcairn back then?"

"During Grandfather Patrick's time, probably about half what it is now. By Earth's standards, its population of eleven thousand people probably sounds pretty small, but it doesn't seem that way to us."

"You mentioned before that this restaurant used to be called the Ivory Street Kitchen. Was that when the government ran it?"

"Right. Paulina Edelstein managed it and became the owner after the transition. It was named after her, of course, and the name stuck after she died."

Goldstein nodded, looking around the dining room. The thick wooden beams and columns, carved from native trees, were worn but still looked more than capable of bearing up under Pitcairn's extreme weather and gravity. Noticing their food was on the way, he leaned back in his chair.

"Here you are, Bryan. Ambassador." Jean Menzies placed their plates in front of them. "Pitcairn chili for you, Administrator, and a steak, baked potato, and broccoli for you, Ambassador." Goldstein could have sworn she held his gaze for a moment longer than usual as she set his plate down. They held out their hands, and Jean used a small chip reader to record their meals. Goldstein's meal would be charged to the Terran Embassy; Bryan, like all Pitcairn leaders, was a Ward of the State during his time in office and would not be paying.

"Still sticking with Earth food, I see," Bryan said.

"As if a good steak was that easy to get on Earth," Goldstein answered. "Better this than that scorching stuff you're eating. And for breakfast!"

Bryan grinned. "I guess you've got to be a native Pitcairner to appreciate a dish with a little spiciness. Paulina invented this dish back in my great-grandfather's time. For years, this was the only place you could get it."

"Are you sure she wasn't pranking you all?"

Bryan laughed. "She knew how to cater to our tastes. Maybe Jean could teach you to appreciate Grissom cuisine."

"Jean? Our server? I've tried to get her to call me Ed, but she insists on calling me Ambassador. I thought Pitcairners were more informal."

"She's trying to impress you. Or get your attention. I'm not sure which. Maybe both."

Goldstein was genuinely puzzled. "Why?"

"Damned if I know. But she is about your age and single."

Goldstein looked across the room where Jean Menzies was coming out of the kitchen with another order. "She's single? An attractive woman her age?"

Bryan shrugged. "She's tall for a Pitcairner. Taller than most Pitcairn men. I guess that's a little intimidating."

"Hmm. I find Pitcairn women to be rather short, mostly. Jean is more like the women I'm used to." He stared across the room, suddenly aware of possibilities he hadn't considered before.

Bryan interrupted his reverie. "You do have one good diplomatic skill."

Goldstein turned back to his friend. "What skill is that?"

"You've distracted me from asking more about why you're unhappy about going back to Earth. I'm pretty sure it's not because you'll miss Pitcairn."

Goldstein shook his head and smiled. "Not distracting enough, apparently. You kept the subject in mind."

"That's right. So, what is bothering you?"

"It's probably nothing. I don't know why Romero wants me to come with him." His fingers were tapping again. "Of course, I don't know what the mission is, so I don't have any reason to think he doesn't need me."

"But you think his reasons may not be good ones?"

"I don't know. I would take over the embassy while Romero was gone if I stayed. I'm senior to Herrara, although not by much, and he may be pushing Herrara ahead of me."

Bryan rubbed his chin. "I do get the impression he doesn't like you much." He grinned at Goldstein. "What did you do to him?"

Goldstein grimaced. "Nothing that I know of. I'm a northerner, though."

"A northerner?"

"Pitcairn was founded by a ship from the old United States. After the Yellowstone Event, it lost its dominant position, and the Western Alliance formed mostly from southern countries. Some southerners look down on people from the northern districts, perhaps a remnant of bad feelings from when the north looked down on the south."

"That was centuries ago," Bryan said. "That kind of bigotry wouldn't still exist, would it?"

Goldstein's smile was more grim than amused. "Pitcairn is a different world. I assure you, that kind of bigotry can still exist on Earth."

"After your success in the Transpacific talks with Japan before you came here, I would think he would appreciate you more."

Goldstein nodded, but there was no conviction in it. "I'm afraid my ancestry counts for more than my successes in diplomatic circles." He paused. "If I'd known what it would be like, I probably would have chosen another line of work."

Bryan smiled. "But then we wouldn't be sitting here enjoying this meal."

Goldstein returned the smile. "There is that." But the smile faded quickly.